"What the hel a baby?"

The infant took one [...] the room, and let out a startled yell. "I'm holding him, that's what," Annie snapped. "They've been a little cranky."

"'They'?"

Annie started to pace, trying to soothe the baby and at the same time contain her growing anger towards Cal. "Your other baby is in the next room. They're twins."

"Wait. Hold it a minute. What do you mean *my* other baby?"

"The mother says you didn't know, but surely you suspected." Annie took advantage of a lull in the child's screams to lower her voice into a tight stern tone. "But whether you knew or not, we still have two babies to deal with. Two babies. Two," she repeated, as if that made him twice as guilty.

"This is unbelievable. A misunderstanding..." Cal massaged his temples with his fingertips as if to clear his head.

"The only misunderstanding is that, after last night, I hoped I might be part of your life," she blurted out. "What a fool! From now on I'm staying out of your personal life—and out of your bed."

Dear Reader

Madeline Harper really enjoys writing humour.
With their new Temptation novel, *The Trouble
with Babies*, this author team has created the
ultimate recipe for comedy. They took a hero
and heroine who are totally incompatible, put
them in an outrageous situation and added
adorable twin babies. Then, as they say, "We
mixed all these ingredients together to see what
would happen." The result is a comedy lover's
delight!

As a reviewer in the magazine *Affaire de Coeur*
has said

  "Madeline Harper is a master of romantic
  comedy…"

Please do write and let us know what you feel
about the books we are selecting for you in
Temptation.

Happy reading!

The Editor
Mills & Boon Temptation
Eton House
18-24 Paradise Road
Richmond
Surrey
TW9 1SR

THE TROUBLE WITH BABIES

BY

MADELINE HARPER

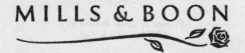

MILLS & BOON

*All the characters in this book have no existence outside the imagination
of the author, and have no relation whatsoever to anyone bearing the
same name or names. They are not even distantly inspired by any
individual known or unknown to the author, and all the incidents are
pure invention.*

*MILLS & BOON and the Rose Device are trademarks of the publisher.
TEMPTATION is a trademark of Harlequin Enterprises II B.V., used
under licence.
First published in Great Britain in 1995
by Harlequin Mills & Boon Limited, Eton House, 18-24 Paradise Road,
Richmond, Surrey TW9 1SR*

© Madeline Porter and Shannon Harper 1995

ISBN 0 263 79454 7

21 - 9510

*Printed in Great Britain by
BPC Paperbacks Ltd*

1

"FITS LIKE A GLOVE."

Cal Markam leaned back in his father's deep leather office chair, a satisfied smile on his face. He swung his feet onto the mahogany desk top and toyed with the idea of smoking one of his father's cigars. He even reached for the deeply carved humidor and then changed his mind. Better wait to celebrate with the old man. After all, that must be why Cal had been called back to Philadelphia. J.C. Markam was ready to step down as CEO of Markam Investments and leave the way clear for his number one son. His only son. John Calvin Markam IV.

Cal pushed up the sleeve of his brown leather bomber jacket to check his watch only to find he wasn't wearing one. Had he left the Rolex beside the hot tub in Malibu? Or maybe on the yacht in Newport Beach? Or at the private gym in Beverly Hills? He wasn't worried. He could always buy a new one.

Cal chuckled as he remembered his last few days in Southern California, the mad scene of farewell dinners and parties with old friends and new acquaintances. He left L.A. in a champagne haze of sleepless nights and sun-filled days and flew directly into a Philadelphia downpour.

The office door opened, and a slight, ramrod-straight figure strode in. "That's not your desk yet so remove your feet, please."

"Good to see you, too, Dad."

J.C. studied his son through narrowed blue eyes. "You look like something the cat dragged in."

Cal couldn't help smiling. His father had always been into corny sayings; it was kind of comforting to hear one again. But he didn't hesitate to unfold himself from his father's chair and move aside to let J.C. settle in.

"When did you last see a barber?"

Cal pushed his shoulder-length hair back from his face and shrugged. "Too busy."

"Or a shave?" J.C. snapped.

"All in good time, Dad. I'm kind of easing back into the Philadelphia life-style. Remember, I just got in this morning."

"*You* remember there's a big difference between the City of Brotherly Love and the City of Angels. I've always thought Los Angeles was misnamed. Now I'm beginning to believe Philadelphia is, too. It's become a real dog-eat-dog city."

Cal mulled that over as he settled into a Victorian chair near the window. "But that's not what you brought me here to talk about."

"No, it's not. This is a family matter. I may be only sixty-five, a man in his prime, but your mother says it's time to retire."

"I've heard the rumor."

"Well, it's a rumor no longer. She's moving to Florida this winter with or without me. Has her sights set on a Palm Beach condo and even signed us up for some damned New Year's cruise."

Cal bit back a smile. He knew very well that his tough businessman father was putty in the hands of his mother, the diminutive and dainty Sarah Markam.

"So, I'm going to retire. But you'd already guessed that. It's why you're here, right, son?"

"You called. I came."

J.C. almost chuckled. "You don't always rush home when I call. This time is different."

Cal knew what was coming. The passing of the mantle. The moment for his father to announce that everything was in order for John Calvin Markam IV to take over as captain of the far-flung Markam Investments empire. Cal managed to look somewhat sheepish.

But J.C. wasn't buying it. In fact, he seemed to have something else on his mind as he fiddled with a pen on his desk, frowning slightly. Then he raised his eyes slowly to Cal's. "Son, I don't know any way to say it but straight, just like I always have. You know I want you to head up the firm. It's what we've always planned, but . . ."

Cal tensed. "I don't like the sound of that *but*, Dad."

"Don't blame you, son. I'm not fond of it myself. So, I'd better explain everything, starting with that damned Board of Directors."

"The Board?"

"And your Aunt Dee."

So that was it. His father's sister, never Cal's biggest fan.

"She and some others on the Board plan to fight your appointment as CEO. She's mounting an all-out campaign for your cousin Glen to step into my shoes."

Cal shook his head. Surely, he'd heard wrong. Glen? Dee's weasel-faced son, who did nothing but echo all of J.C.'s pronouncements? "Good Lord, Dad. Glen hasn't had an original thought in twenty years. He lacks creativity, originality and imagination. He'd be death to Markam Investments. He'd—"

J.C. interrupted his son. "You don't have to tell me that, son. I have no great affection for Glen. But consider this—he has the right education, the right experience and, more importantly, the right image. While you've been prancing around like a colt, he's been a real workhorse at Markam."

There were the quaint expressions again, but this time Cal wasn't amused. "I know you were disappointed when I didn't join the company right out of grad school, but I wanted to bring more than classroom claptrap to my work. *You* encouraged me to be my own man, to be independent."

"Not that you needed much encouragement, son. You've always been as stubborn as a mule."

"To quote one of your proverbs, 'The apple doesn't fall far from the tree.' Stubbornness seems to run in the family. But I believed—and still do—that I needed a diversity of experience before joining Markam Investments."

J.C. gave a derisive snort. "By diversity do you mean running around California with Surfer Babes and nudie housecleaners?"

"They weren't nude, and you know it," Cal corrected. "You've seen spreadsheets on my surfing company and on Bikini Kleen. In six years, I took those companies from nothing—less than nothing—and put them on the map. I've proven myself in the business world, which is a hell of a lot more than Glen has done hanging around Markam Investments acting as a yesman."

"The Board knows all about the success of your business ventures in California."

Cal shrugged and tried to show a semblance of humility.

"And readers of those sleazy tabloids know even more about your personal life."

Cal looked away, out the window.

"That's the problem, son. You made money, but you missed the point along the way. The image that you created was hardly one that the Board of Directors of Markam Investments would approve of."

"Image shouldn't count more than accomplishments," Cal argued.

J.C. raised a sardonic eyebrow. "I wish that were true. But the fact is, image counts for a great deal, especially here in Philadelphia where your Aunt Dee is one of society's darlings."

"Darling is hardly the word I'd use to describe her."

J.C. stifled a smile. "Whatever the term, about half the members of our Board are in her camp. She has convinced them that your past publicity and questionable life-style will interfere with Markam's image."

Cal made a noise deep in his throat.

"Don't snicker, son. Your Aunt Dee makes the valid point that we could lose some of our oldest and most valuable and—I might add—wealthiest clients because of your past indiscretions."

"There's another ridiculous term. My *indiscretions* damage the firm's image? I can't be responsible for tabloid exaggeration."

J.C. leaned back in his chair and looked his son straight in the eye. "Exaggeration? Do you deny the parties, the women, the..." J.C. grimaced as if in pain.

Cal shrugged and said stubbornly, "It has nothing to do with my ability to run Markam."

"The damage is done," J.C. barked. "All we can do is try to pick up the pieces. Frankly, I can swing some of the Board my way, but not all of them."

"Damn, this makes me mad." Cal got up and began to pace the office. He had always planned someday to take his place at Markam Investments. He'd built his whole life around that dream. Part of it, he'd done his parents' way—his Ivy League education, his masters degree in business. His internship—as he considered it—in the rough-and-tumble world of California entrepreneurship had been his own idea. But it had been aimed at gathering experience to run Markam.

"Maybe Southern California wasn't the ideal training ground," J.C. observed dryly. "Too many temptations."

"I made a lot of money. I earned my stripes in the business world."

"Some people don't call surfboards 'business.'"

Cal turned to face his father. "Then some people are misinformed. I bought a surfboard manufacturing company that was in trouble and turned it into a major corporation."

"What about Surfer Babes and Dudes?"

"Those were the teams that I sponsored to advertise my surfboards. They gave me all the right pointers for improving the boards. I came up with the best product, and then I branched off into swimsuits and sun products. Why not? It was a natural."

"But the image of those women in skimpy swimsuits..."

Cal grinned. "So you noticed? Hell, by the time the company went public, no one was asking questions about the image. My surfers were pulling down acting and modeling jobs, and my products were in every shop on both coasts, not to mention Hawaii, Australia—"

"All right. Maybe I picked a bad example with your first company, but your next venture was a disaster—"

"Disaster? I made a fortune with Bikini Kleen."

J.C. cringed.

"You might not like the name, but it certainly is catchy."

"Cal, my boy, that's hardly the word. Can you imagine the Markam Board approving a CEO who posed for photographs with naked men and women holding mops and buckets?"

Cal couldn't hold back his laughter. "Dad, I bought a failing cleaning company, hired enthusiastic, energetic young people—struggling actors who looked good in swimsuits—and sent them out to clean houses. One guy and one gal per house. And they weren't naked. In fact, they were very well clad—"

"In bikinis?"

"They did a great job. It was an added plus that they looked sensational. Anyhow, we're in franchise now, and I'm out of it."

"What about the surfers?"

"Turned a big profit and left the business for my partner, Rick Johnson, to run. He's done a great job, and I'm out of that, too."

"Completely?"

Cal threw up his hands in despair. "Okay. I kept an interest in some of the product lines, Surfer Babes and Dudes tanning lotion, for example. But it's just on paper."

J.C. swiveled around in his chair. "Why couldn't you have tried real estate or automotive parts or even oranges? They grow oranges in California."

"You know why, Dad. I enjoy women. In fact, I love them. Oranges just didn't interest me."

"Ah, yes. Women. Sad to say, the Board has your career documented from the first time you stepped onto the sand in Southern California—a place, I might add, for which no one in Philadelphia has any respect at all. It follows that—"

"They have no respect for me."

"You said it, son."

"Even if for all practical purposes I'm out of it?"

"But are you out of it?" J.C. asked. "Your Aunt Dee has gotten a bee in her bonnet about the kind of folks you associate with, especially your woman friends. The kind who get you in the tabloids."

Cal was incensed. "Bee in her bonnet or not, the people I choose as friends are none of her business."

"Personally, no. Professionally, yes. And it's the professional aspect we're discussing now, Cal. Dee isn't sure your friends are appropriate types for the CEO of a company like Markam. She's worried about—" J.C. set his jaw in a very Main Line fashion and spoke through clenched teeth in a perfect imitation of his sister "—embarrassing episodes that might damage the company."

Cal let a brief smile cross his face in memory of a few of those episodes. If she'd witnessed them, poor Aunt Dee would have fainted dead away. Cal gazed at his father intensely. "My friends are loyal to me, as I am to them. I can't help it if most of them are high profile show-business types. That's the kind of people I met in my line of work. I didn't run into any little old ladies from Philadelphia's Main Line whose main concern is whether or not to roll over their C.D.s."

Suddenly J.C. became defensive. "Those little old ladies are Markam customers, son. They turn their money over to us and expect that we'll invest it wisely and make even more. I might remind you that if you want to take over this company, you should be respectful of them."

Cal bit back his response. High on his agenda for Markam reform was to broaden its base of investors, and to do it soon—before the existing clients were all dead! There was a wide world of wealth out there, people who never had heard of the Main Line and couldn't have cared less about its social mores. Markam hadn't begun to scratch the surface of its potential market.

"Glen can't do it," Cal muttered.

"What?"

"He can't lead Markam into the 21st Century. Changes have to be made, and unless I'm running the company they might never happen. Glen can't keep Markam competitive. I can."

Having said his piece, Cal moved away from the window and took a seat on the divan opposite his father's desk. It was upholstered in a discreet floral pattern. Very Victorian and safe, like the rest of the room. Like the rest of the company.

J.C. reached for the humidor and carefully selected a cigar. He rolled it between his fingers thoughtfully before lighting it. "Smoke?" he asked Cal.

Cal shook his head.

"I know it's time for a change, son. Our accounting needs to be streamlined, our investment portfolios need to be broadened. I wanted to take charge of the transformation myself, but your mother had other plans. Besides, it may be too late for me. However, it's the right time for you. I have no doubt you can take on all the challenges."

Cal felt a sigh escape his lips.

"But first you have to get past the Board, and that's not going to be an easy task."

"I understand that, Dad."

"Are you committed to this fight, heart and soul?"

"I want the job," Cal said evenly.

"On any terms?" J.C.'s blue eyes were sharp and canny.

He met his father's look. "Possibly. But maybe I should hear what you have in mind before I commit."

"The Board meets in two months, right after Thanksgiving." J.C. puffed on the cigar. "You have that long to turn your image around."

"Dad, not that again."

Suddenly J.C. stood up and stretched to his full height. "Let me tell you something, Cal. I'm damned tired of picking up tabloids and reading about my son the ladies' man, the adventurer, the party boy. Mr. Good Time, Mr. Big Time."

Cal set his chin stubbornly. "I only did what you did years before, Dad. Finished university and graduate school, and then took a few years off to enjoy life and indulge a few fantasies. Now I'm back home, and I'm ready for Markam."

"There's a big difference between your actions and mine. Or those of my father or even my grandfather. We kicked over the traces, certainly, but we didn't do it *publicly*. J.C. spat out the word. "We sowed our wild oats in Europe or the South Seas, privately, discreetly, like gentlemen, not for the press—and therefore the whole damned world—to find out about."

Cal nodded wordlessly and waited for the rest of the tirade.

"Furthermore, I'm tired of having Dee remind me that your exploits are common knowledge. Maybe none of it means a damned thing. But I'd like for a change to pick up the *Wall Street Journal* or the *New York Times* and read about my son the humanitarian, the art lover, the benefactor. I'd like to see a photo of you *without* a blonde on your arm."

Cal grinned. "I don't discriminate, Dad. I like brunettes and redheads, too."

"It's not a laughing matter, son." J.C. sat back down. "Two paternity suits in six years aren't funny."

Cal's grin faded. "You don't believe that trash, do you?"

"I don't want to, but where there's smoke . . ."

Cal's jaw tightened. "The subject is closed. I handled those suits, and there's no point dredging them up again."

J.C. sighed. "I don't think your Aunt Dee sees it that way. Dammit it, son, we need a drastic change in your public image. I know you can turn yourself around, but I can't swing the Board to your side unless you prove it. You have two months to make it happen."

"That's a hell of a tall order. I can do it, of course," he added quickly, his mind coursing. "I just need to make a few adjustments here and there in my lifestyle—"

"Adjustments, hell! More like major surgery." J.C. reached into his desk, took out a business card and handed it to his son.

"Bert Canelli, Public Relations/Image Consultation," Cal read. "PR? You can't be serious!"

"At this point, I see no other way. Canelli is one of the best in the business—"

"Aunt Dee would love that tidbit. I can hear her now, 'Cal's had to hire someone to make him acceptable to the Board.' It won't fly, Dad. Just more ammunition to be used against me. I'm so tainted, you had to hire Bert Canelli to whip me into shape? No way."

"Do you seriously believe I didn't think of that, Cal? Obviously, I've explained everything to Bert. He understands the situation, and he has someone who can handle everything privately and discreetly. She's new to the area, not yet known in Philadelphia, and she's a crackerjack, Bert tells me."

Cal sank deep into the divan. "She?"

"That's right. You can pass her off as your assistant or secretary or whatever, if you happen to be seen together. Dee and the Board will be none the wiser. I'm not even going to mention the PR firm to your mother. She can be as surprised as everyone else when you make the transformation from playboy to solid citizen."

"I don't like the idea of someone else running my life, making my decisions," Cal growled. "I can handle this image thing myself, Dad."

J.C.'s reply was firm. "Not a chance. We do it my way or not at all. I sent a box full of clippings on the life-style of Cal Markam to the PR firm. A box full! Every story seemed to be accompanied by photos of you and at least one scantily clad woman, followed by some damn story about your love life."

"I don't control the press."

"Then try to control yourself. Since you can't seem to do it alone, you need professional help." He extinguished his cigar and glanced at his watch. "Your appointment is in half an hour."

2

THE RAIN WAS coming down in torrents, and Annie Valentine was stuck in traffic two blocks from her office. To make matters worse, she was late for an important appointment.

She cut in front of the truck that was creating the problems, ignored the cursing driver, and just made the light. She cut off another truck to get into the right hand lane. More curses. Trucks weren't her thing today, but she didn't have time to worry about it. Cal Markam was probably getting very impatient cooling his heels in the reception room.

Annie turned into the underground parking lot, drove to her space and turned off the engine. What a day! And the worst was yet to come.

Annie decided to stay in the car for a couple of minutes to get her mind focused on the Markam account. When Bert Canelli had told her about Cal and his problems, she'd looked forward to the challenge of reforming his bad boy image. Until Bert slipped in the clincher. She couldn't take credit, at least not publicly, for Cal's transformation. Annie was ambitious and liked recognition. Bert knew that, and to allay her disappointment, he promised not only a raise but a shot at the next superstar client who walked through the door—*if* she was successful with Cal, and J.C. Markam got what he wanted.

And if she failed? Annie couldn't waste energy thinking about that. She was determined to be successful. Her boss wasn't known for harboring failures. He'd made it clear that they were all winners at Canelli. He'd entrusted her with an important client, and since being fired wouldn't enhance her résumé, she had to succeed. It was that simple.

She checked her reflection in the rearview mirror and ran a comb quickly through her hair. Another car pulled into the space next to her. Bert's space. She glanced over and saw a man in a bomber jacket, the bill of his baseball cap shadowing his face. Definitely not Bert, but he didn't seem concerned that he was parking in a private place. Of course, Bert was out of town but the usurper couldn't know that. *Arrogant*, she thought as she got out of the car and headed for her office.

ANNIE STEPPED OFF the elevator only to find the reception room empty. "Where is he?"

"Hasn't shown yet," the receptionist said.

Annie gave a sigh of relief and headed for her office. There'd be time to make some calls. She sat down at her desk, looked through her messages, and reached for the phone just as it rang.

"Mr. Markam is here, Ms. Valentine," the receptionist informed her.

Annie stood up, smoothed the pants of her black silk suit and buttoned the jacket over her forest green blouse. "No need to be nervous," she lectured herself.

"Remember, you function best under pressure. He's just another client. . . ."

But she *was* nervous. So much was riding on how she handled this account. She took a deep breath and opened the door to face the arrogant—and, she realized immediately, devastatingly handsome—man who had usurped Bert's parking place.

"It's you." God, what a dumb thing to say, Annie thought.

"Yep. The guy from the parking lot. I watched you walk away from your car, and I thought to myself that redheads have a very different way of moving. The redheaded walk, I call it."

Annie pretended she hadn't heard his remark and held out her hand. "I'm Annie Valentine."

He took her hand in both of his and smiled ingratiatingly. "John Calvin Markam, IV, showing up for inspection, as requested." He gave her fingers a little squeeze, but didn't release his grip.

"A brief handshake will do, Mr. Markam," she said, extricating herself and trying not to think about the warmth and strength of his grasp, "and you're a little late for your inspection." Annie masked her nervousness by taking charge. Doing her best to ignore his broad shoulders, long legs, slim hips and eyes that were bluer than blue, she looked askance at the baseball cap, earring and mane of long hair. "And we have a problem."

"If we didn't, I wouldn't be here, would I?"

"Point well taken. Come in, please."

Cal crossed the room in three long strides, stripped off his bomber jacket and dropped it on a chair.

As Annie surveyed his T-shirt—purple with a Surfer Babes and Dudes logo featuring a bikinied blonde caressing her surfboard—she couldn't help but notice the broad chest beneath it. And, although she disapproved of the long brown hair that tumbled over his forehead, she couldn't overlook its shine and tawny gold highlights. Both clothes and hair would have to change.

Annie sat down, gaining confidence behind her solid cherry desk with its executive appearance. She watched him settle in comfortably, cross an ankle on one knee and rest his cap on the other. "So, you're the new kid on the block?"

That was a jolt to her self-assurance. She fought to regain it. "If you mean I'm new to Philadelphia, that's true, which is why I was chosen for your case. However, I can assure you that I've had appropriate experience...."

Cal nodded, waiting for her résumé.

"University of Pittsburgh, PR firm in Harrisburg. Now Philadelphia. I guess you could say I've worked my way across the state, west to east."

"Upward and onward, eh? I can relate."

"Good. Now, back to the PR campaign—"

"Do you like Philly?"

"So far, it's fine," she said quickly. "Now, let's—"

"Getting to know the city? Making friends?"

Exasperated, she frowned. "We're talking about you, Mr. Markam."

"You can't blame me for being curious about the woman whose hands I'm in—in a matter of speaking." His eyes gleamed mischievously.

"I've only been in town three months, and I've spent most of that time working."

"Too bad. All work and no play—"

It was her turn to interrupt. "Mr. Markam, you're way off the subject."

"Cal. I'm Cal, and you're Annie. Deal?" He smiled. It was a fabulous smile, Annie noticed. Little laugh lines appeared around his eyes, and his teeth flashed white and straight. A billion-dollar smile, she thought. But the rest of his appearance was considerably less expensive. Besides the T-shirt and baseball cap, he sported worn jeans and scuffed-up sneakers. Not an ideal look for a potential CEO of a staid Fortune 500 company. What had possessed him to dress like this for a business interview?

"It's a deal—Cal," she responded firmly. "Now, let's get down to business." She picked up a file.

"I'm delighted to be working with you instead of Bert."

"You know Bert?"

Cal shook his head. "No, but I guarantee you've got better legs."

Annie had the feeling that Cal Markam knew only one way to relate to women, but he would have to learn that *this* woman was different. Clients had flirted with her before, and she always handled the situation with dispatch and finesse. Of course, none of her clients was as physically overwhelming as Cal. "Mr. Markam, please—"

"Cal, remember?"

"I'll call you Cal if you'll respect my position. You've hired me to change your image—"

"My dad hired you," Cal corrected.

"But you're here, aren't you?"

"Point well taken," he said, repeating her earlier words.

"Then we'll get to work." She picked up the file again, satisfied with its weight. She'd done her research well.

"You mean we're starting today? I thought this was the get-acquainted session."

She looked up. "We are acquainted."

"But I just flew in—"

"We have only two months." She spoke with a sense of urgency. "Two months to change your total image. I'm very good at my job, but I can't work miracles."

He chuckled. "I'm in that much trouble, huh?"

Annie frowned. She hadn't expected repentance, but she was disturbed to find that Cal was amused by his reputation. She opened the file.

"Is that the stuff Dad sent over?"

"Oh, no." She indicated a box of clippings on her desk. "Your press coverage is in there. My file includes research I've done on my own."

"I see. You work very fast. Or did Dad put this plan in action a long time ago?"

"I've had only a few days."

"Then you *are* good. But that's been established already."

"Yes, Mr.—uh, Cal—it has. And now it's time to talk about you." Finally, she thought. "While we're on the subject of your press clippings, let's start there. You've been very busy."

"Why do I have the feeling you don't approve of the press I've been getting?"

"Let me ask the questions, please."

He shrugged.

"Do you understand the problem you've created in terms of Markam Investments?"

"I believe so, but maybe you should go over it for me."

Annie ignored the sarcasm. And the glint of laughter in his blue eyes. "People reading these clips might see you as a playboy, and if I may be blunt, an exploiter of women."

"Hold on. I can understand that people might think of me as a playboy. I do like to play, but on the other hand, I'm not a boy," he added with a grin. "And I've certainly never exploited women."

Annie bit back a sharp retort. She'd hold off on the paternity suits until she laid her groundwork. She pulled out a clipping of Cal and two bikini-clad Surfer Babes. "Just the name of your team in itself—"

"Time out again," he interrupted. "Those are very savvy men *and* women who knew how to use publicity to get ahead. Let's just say I created employment for healthy, attractive young people."

"Especially young, nubile females," Annie muttered as she scribbled a few notes.

Cal's mouth quirked in a half smile. "Some of the women hit it big time. A couple are in movies now, and another is an international model. You might even say I discovered her. Her name's Charley. You probably have photos of her—the tall blonde. She was in lots of our ad campaigns."

Annie remembered the model, a standout among a field of beauties. Now a household name in the fashion world.

"Charley's an example of how my company gave its employees opportunities. She started as a Surfer Babe, modeled in our campaigns . . ."

"And had dozens of photos taken with you." Annie riffled through the clippings.

"She knew the value of good PR—being seen with me!"

At Annie's astonished look, he laughed. "Just joking."

"Did you date her?" The moment the question popped out, she knew it wasn't appropriate.

Cal didn't seem to mind. "Yeah, I went out with her a few times, but mostly Charley, Rick and I hung out together. Rick was my partner, who's running things now." There was a faraway look in Cal's eyes. "The three of us had some good times. Once I remember—"

"I think we'll downplay your good times with models like this . . . Charley," Annie interrupted. "Fortunately, I'll be able to put a positive spin on some of your other activities such as the balloon trip over Africa, rafting down the Colorado, mountain climbing in Chile—" She looked up at him. "You do whatever appeals to you?"

"If I can fit it in, sure. Why not? Life is short, and I want to enjoy it all."

"You've done a good job so far," Annie commented dryly. "But some of it won't hurt our case because I've been able to slant some of those experiences in a way that will show you not as a playboy jet-setter but as a daring adventurer. You like the outdoors?"

"Obviously."

"Then it's only a short step to environmentalist."

He shifted in his chair, and Annie saw that he was uncomfortable with that. "I don't belong to any of those groups," he told her.

"But you don't do anything to harm the environment. In fact, you try to protect it as best you can?"

"Of course."

"Then it's time for you to speak out on the issue," she said firmly.

"By 'speak out,' I suppose you mean make speeches, join the movements."

"That's part of my plan. I imagine you'll be a very good speaker," Annie encouraged.

"Well, why not? As long as I can mention that I like indoor sports, too," he added with a grin.

Annie frowned again. "That is exactly the kind of remark we need to be careful about. Some people might construe it as macho and sexual."

Cal raised his eyebrows in mock surprise. "I can't imagine why they would! I meant racquetball, pool, bowling. You didn't think I was referring to sex as an indoor sport, did you?"

Annie felt her cheeks flush. He had set her up and was enjoying her discomfort. Unfortunately, she couldn't control the flare of color in her face. "I don't know you well enough to know what you meant," she countered.

"That will change." He glanced at her intently. "You really shouldn't frown so much, Annie. Eventually you'll get those little lines between your eyes—"

Annie slapped the file shut. "You're not serious about this, are you? It's all just a game to you."

The teasing glint disappeared from Cal's eyes. He leaned forward, invading her space, and Annie pushed back in her chair. Cal was exuding a fierce power, very different from his earlier easygoing demeanor. There was no doubt that he was a Markam, cut from the same cloth as his father, a man who liked to be in charge and always got what he wanted.

"Yeah, I think it's a game. I know, and my father and even my aunt know, that I could take over Markam Investments tomorrow and run it damned well. But since some of the Board members are hung up on appearance and image and overblown publicity, I have to dance around like a trained monkey to prove what everybody already knows."

"Yet you *are* going to go through with it?"

"I want the job, and I want it badly enough to play out this charade. What I'm hoping is that you can make my transformation happen as quickly and painlessly as possible. A nice shiny surface gloss—"

"So you see what I'm doing as purely cosmetic?"

"What else? No matter what your skills, you can't change a person in two months. Not real change. So, what else is left but the surface?"

"I don't agree with you," Annie said. "We all have the power to change, and I see myself as helping facilitate that change. I've done it before. It's part of my job."

"Maybe you've been fooled by your clients, Annie."

She bristled. "Or maybe my clients really wanted to change."

Cal leaned back in the chair, his smile sardonic. "Well, I don't want to. I just want you to convince the Board that I have. Can you do that, Ms. Annie Valentine?"

"I can do whatever has to be done," Annie said firmly. "Maybe we have different approaches, but we have the same goal, don't we?"

"For the Board to vote in my favor? Yes."

"Then let me show you some of the ideas I've come up with. That way I think you'll get a better understanding of how I work." She moved to a chart in the corner of her office and flipped over the first page. "You don't have to take notes," she instructed. "I've had the presentation printed out for you."

Cal hadn't given a thought to taking notes, and looking at Annie Valentine, he didn't know whether to laugh or cry.

She wasn't at all what he had expected after first seeing her. When she got out of the car in the parking lot, he'd been struck by how attractive she was. Not drop-dead gorgeous like some of the Surfer Babes but definitely good-looking. Her nose was small and straight, her mouth wide and generous, and she had golden brown eyes the color of good sherry. Her hair was a little short for his taste, but it was a fabulous red color and framed her features nicely. When he'd watched her walk away in the parking lot, he had been able to tell that she was nicely curved in the places that mattered. From the rear, anyway. Now he observed the line of her full breasts and narrow waist. Front and back, there was a firm but curvy body under that silk. He imagined her working out regularly, not enjoying it, but doing it because she appreciated the results. So did Cal.

But there was a problem. She came across as a mixture of drill sergeant and Sunday school teacher. Her sense of humor was nonexistent—she was far too serious for Cal, who liked women playful and flirtatious. Not to mention a little wild. But could there be some fun under that businesslike demeanor? He doubted it. Some women came across as serious until they got a chance for a little adventure, and then they really let go. He couldn't imagine Annie was one of them.

"I've divided the campaign strategy into a three-point attack," Annie was saying. She flipped another page. "First— "

Cal interrupted. "Campaign? Strategy? Attack? You make this sound like a war."

"Oh, it is," Annie replied earnestly. "And most of it will be fought in the trenches, hand-to-hand combat. The enemies—your aunt and her cohorts—will fire the first volleys, bring up your past, try to smear you. Then we'll fire back by staging a spectacular event, something that clearly shows you're a new man. We'll outgun them with favorable press, outflank them with superior strategy."

"Is there a restaurant in this building?"

"A what?" Annie looked at him with the beginning of a frown which she quickly halted and then wished she hadn't. It wasn't a good idea to be caught taking his advice.

"A restaurant," he repeated.

"Yes, there is, on the first floor. That has nothing to do with our strategy, Cal."

"Maybe not, but what do you say to lunch?"

"No, I—"

"Annie, if I'm going to get through the rest of this presentation, I'll need some nourishment. I haven't eaten since yesterday unless you count the so-called continental breakfast on the plane. Have pity on me."

"But the charts?"

"You printed out a copy for me. I bet you have another one in your file."

"Yes, but—"

"You can read from that. I'll follow carefully. Do this for me, Annie, before I die of starvation."

ANNIE SIPPED HER COFFEE, ate a salad and watched Cal devour a three-course meal. When he finished and leaned back she took that as a signal to proceed. "If you'll turn to the second page..." she said.

Cal did as he was told before waving the waiter over for more coffee. "The lunch crowd has gone. I'm sure they won't mind us staying for a while," he said.

"I'm counting on it," Annie answered. "Now, you'll notice on page two, the ecological plan I mentioned." She paused while the waiter poured their coffee.

"What about dessert?" Cal asked her.

Annie shook her head.

"I think I'll have a crème brûlée," Cal told the waiter. Then to Annie, "I can read and eat dessert at the same time. Go ahead."

"Besides speaking for the cause that we'll choose and appearing at fund-raisers, you'll need to make a contribution."

"I'll be contributing my time."

"I mean a monetary contribution. That's the quickest way to get on the boards of these charities. I'm assuming money isn't a problem?"

"No problem. But consult me before choosing an environmental cause, Annie. I might as well be interested in what I'm contributing to."

"There'll be more than one charitable group," she warned. "I'd like to include a cultural organization, a theater or dance company, maybe a children's art museum."

"Me and children? No way. Besides, children hardly fit my image," he replied sarcastically.

Annie managed a sweet smile. "And that image is just what we're trying to change."

Cal's crème brûlée arrived and he dug in, still listening as Annie outlined his options. This was one of the craziest things he'd ever done, Cal mused, but what were his choices? Maybe he could have won over the Board on his own; he liked to take chances, liked risks. But he didn't want to alienate J.C., who seemed to have faith in this PR thing.

As she talked, Annie turned a page so Cal quickly did the same. He needed to play along with her, meet her halfway, make a few appearances and garner some good press. He didn't expect it would take two months. Maybe less than six weeks to achieve the necessary surface sheen. But could he put up with Annie and her charts and outlines for that long? Not unless she lightened up, he decided.

She turned another page, and he followed suit. "Any questions?" she asked.

"No, I can't imagine there's anything left to cover."

"Then we'll move on to presentation. Your appearance," she clarified.

She was really into this, Cal thought. He enjoyed his work, but Annie brought an intensity to hers that was almost manic. He wondered what drove her, what she was trying to prove.

"I assume you have a suitable wardrobe," she said.

"What I lack, I'll have my father's tailor whip up for me. Conservative suits, right? Pale blue shirts and striped ties? No sneakers."

"That sounds fine." She should have realized that the son of a wealthy, socially prominent Main Line family was born with good taste. In fact, he was far more well versed than she.

"And there's your hair and your—"

"Earring? I thought maybe I'd wear a diamond stud for the Board appearance and pull my hair into a ponytail."

Annie's response was stern. "I know you're not serious, but it's my job to be thorough."

"Obviously."

She ignored his sarcastic reply and plunged into deeper and more treacherous waters. "Now, about your personal life, you've been linked with a number of women in the press."

"Linked is the correct word. I've never been serious about any of them, but every time I have a date, there's a photo in the papers, and we're considered an item. I've read about my engagement to women I've only met once."

Annie regarded him evenly. Now was the time to face one of the most serious problems head-on. "The paternity suits . . . those were women you only met once?"

Cal returned her gaze coolly. "You go for the jugular, don't you?"

"No matter how uncomfortable it makes me feel, I have to ask, have to be prepared for every contingency. The press loves that kind of story."

He pushed his dessert plate aside. "My standard answer is that to my knowledge, I've never fathered a child. The women involved in those accusations were interested in only one thing—money. The situations were handled discreetly and to everyone's satisfaction, including the lawyers." The traces of a rueful smile broke through. "*Especially* the lawyers."

"Even though you consider the situations handled, they may come up again."

"Then it'll be your job to take care of things, right?"

"If I knew the facts . . ."

"Read the clippings," Cal said brusquely. "I make it a policy not to kiss and tell."

"The women certainly talked."

"They sold their stories to the tabloids before I could stop them. Bottom line, Annie—I didn't even know one of the women and the other—" He shrugged. "We had a brief fling, but as for being the father of her child, the dates were all wrong."

Annie was quiet for a moment, thinking. Whether she believed Cal or not—and she wanted to believe him—he was her client, and it was her business to protect his image.

She could do it. All she needed was his cooperation. "It seems to me the most important thing we need to do is control negative press. I've set up some guidelines, three basic rules—"

"I don't like rules," Cal warned.

"Just look them over, please. This is integral to our success." Annie mentally braced herself for his reaction.

Cal read from the list. "Number one, no interviews with media unless set up by A. Valentine. Number two," he went on, his voice deepening with disbelief. "No dates with anyone not approved by A.V. What the—" Then he saw number three and exploded. "No contact with past friends and acquaintances until after the Board votes!"

He brushed away the waiter's attempt to refill his coffee cup. "Are you crazy, Annie Valentine? If you believe for a minute that you're going to interfere in my private life, you're very wrong." He leaned across the table, his face inches from hers. "Who the hell do you think you are?"

This time Annie didn't back down. She met his gaze evenly, chin thrust out, eyes narrowed. "I'll tell you who I am, *Mr.* Markam. I'm the professional image consultant your father hired to pull your chestnuts out of the fire. Without me you don't have a chance in hell of getting the Markam Board's vote. You've screwed up your image royally, and you need me."

For a long moment they glowered at each other, practically nose-to-nose, neither giving an inch.

Suddenly Cal burst into laughter and leaned back. "Well, well, who would have thought you had all that fire inside? I guess it goes with the red hair." He motioned to the waiter. "Let's have some more coffee."

Annie was embarrassed at her outburst, which had been terribly unprofessional, especially here in the restaurant where she dined frequently. But Cal Markam was so damned infuriating that she hadn't been able to control her frustration.

She fought to regain her composure. "I apologize for losing my temper. That isn't like me at all, but I want to succeed—I mean, I want *you* to succeed," she corrected hastily.

So that's it, Cal thought. Her career was riding on his! No wonder she was so impassioned about her rules and regulations, so enthusiastic about his make-over. Cal studied her thoughtfully. She was energetic and organized, two qualities he admired. And she had just proven that she had heart. He could do worse—professionally, he amended. As for Annie on a personal basis, she was too serious for him.

Annie saw a smile curve his lips and held out her hand. "Then we have a deal?"

Cal took her hand in his.

"You're supposed to shake it," she said.

"You told me that the last time we held hands, Annie." Their eyes met. Hers were velvet soft, deep enough for a man to drown in. Maybe, he thought, way down inside of Ms. Annie Valentine there *could* be a free spirit struggling to break out.

"Yep, I'll try to be a good boy, for as long as I can."

Annie gave a sigh of relief. "That's all I ask." She thought about how warm and strong his hand was, wrapped firmly around hers. Maybe under his teasing and arrogant demeanor, there really was a man of solidity and purpose. She fervently hoped so.

"No interviews unless you set them up," he agreed.

"And I coach you beforehand."

He nodded. "But before we *shake* hands I need to make a couple of things clear. You can approve my public dates, but my private life is off-limits."

"I guess I have no way of knowing what you do behind closed doors."

"Right." Cal grinned. He imagined there'd be a lot Annie wouldn't know. "And as for giving up all my friends—"

"It's only for two short months."

"I may not have many good qualities, but loyalty to old friends tops the list...."

"You can call them," she suggested.

"Are you sure Aunt Dee hasn't tapped my phone?"

"Then send a fax," Annie said with a smile.

"Why, Ms. Valentine, I do believe I detected a note of humor in your last remark." He gave her hand a squeeze.

Annie felt herself blush again.

"So it's a deal." Cal finally shook her hand, which Annie quickly extracted. "What's next?"

"I'll find an ecology issue for you to support. Of course, it's a little difficult to contact people without saying who I am and why I'm calling. And I certainly can't mention Canelli Associates."

"You'll think of something."

"I already have. I'll introduce myself as your assistant, and of course I'll say you've come up with these ideas on your own."

"Sounds good to me." Cal signaled for the check. "I'm staying at my parents' town house on Delancy Place. You can reach me there."

After Cal paid the bill, he took Annie's arm and started to lead her out of the restaurant, but she balked.

"What is it now? Another image problem?"

"Worse," she said. "You forgot your copy of the guidelines and the campaign strategy."

Once again, Cal thought he detected a little humor in Annie's remark. "Slipped my mind," he said gravely, taking the packet from her. "I'll study these at home."

"Great idea. In this business you can't be overprepared."

"My very words," Cal said.

3

FIVE DAYS LATER, Annie climbed out of a taxi in front of the Markam town house, an imposing brick structure, anchored solidly on its quiet tree-lined street and rising four stories high.

Annie looked up and tried to suppress her sense of awe. "Keep the motor running," she told the driver. "We'll be right out."

Her schedule was working out fine. They'd make the plane with plenty of time to spare, and she could brief Cal on the way to the airport and in flight. Not ideal; she would have preferred having him up to speed by now. But Cal was a hard man to pin down, and a few minutes on his answering machine was about all she had been able to manage.

Not that she could have found much more time herself. Annie's days had become increasingly filled as she struggled to set up a comprehensive program for the remaking of Cal Markam.

The remaking of Cal Markam. Annie stopped on the sidewalk and smiled at that. She liked the sound of it.

She pushed open the wrought iron gate and noticed stairs that led down to the basement level where an unobtrusive brass marker indicated Service Only. "Not for me," she said aloud as she headed up to the front door and rang the bell.

Cal's immediate response would have been too much to expect, but that was okay. She was cooking; it was all going to work out.

When the door opened, an attractive gray-haired woman stood before her.

"Mrs. Markam—"

"Goodness, no," the woman replied with a laugh. "Mrs. Markam's at the Bryn Mawr house. I'm Mrs. Batelle, the family's housekeeper."

"Annie Valentine. I have an appointment with Cal."

"Cal's not here right now, but you're welcome to come on in."

"He's not here?" It took a moment for the shock of that information to register, and when it did, Annie kept her calm, willing herself to stay in control. "There must be some mistake," she said evenly. "We have a plane to catch in an hour."

"Oh, my," the housekeeper replied.

"I'm sure he's here and you just haven't seen him," Annie said, looking up at the building. "It's a huge place and—"

"That it is. I know because I supervise the cleaning," she said with a wide smile. "And I can tell you Cal is nowhere to be found in this house, but you come on in and see for yourself." She led Annie to an entranceway that soared to the top floor of the town house. Then she spoke into an intercom. "Lucy, are you there?"

Moments later a voice replied, "I'm in the dining room changing the flowers like you said."

"Fine, Lucy. When did you last see young Mr. Markam?"

"He was here day before yesterday. I believe he went out of town."

Annie's mouth dropped open. Recovering, she said, "She must be mistaken. When I spoke to Cal, he told me to leave the flight information on his answering machine. Which I did. Yesterday. It was very clear. In fact, I left two messages, just in case. . . ." Annie realized she was babbling, but that didn't stop her. "Surely he called in for the message—wherever he was—is," she added weakly since he definitely wasn't here.

"Do you work for one of Cal's companies?"

"No, I—" Annie suddenly remembered the need to keep her real identity a secret. "I'm his assistant. He's scheduled to make a speech later today—in Florida."

Mrs. Batelle's expression wasn't encouraging. "Well, if you really think he's coming, you're welcome to wait in the parlor."

"Thank you." Annie followed the housekeeper into the room where she immediately sank onto a brocade sofa.

"Would you like a cup of coffee?"

"No," Annie said quickly. "I'm nervous enough as it is. But you can do something for me. I have a cab waiting . . ."

"I'll tell the driver to leave."

Well, the housekeeper certainly had no faith in Cal. Neither did Annie. But she had faith in herself, and she'd extracted a promise from him to be here—now. He was late, but there was still time. It wasn't over yet.

"No," she said firmly. "Ask him to wait, please."

As soon as Mrs. Batelle left the room, Annie began to fume. The first damned event she'd planned, and Cal was late. "Damn. Damn," she cursed aloud. They would have to fight traffic to make the flight, fight crowds to get checked in, fight—

If he made it at all. Was it possible that he'd stood her up? The bastard! What if he didn't show? She'd have to make several phone calls to cancel his appearance at the fund-raiser. The event would go on without him, and Cal would get press, all right, tons of *negative* press about being a no-show and ruining the big day. Her first event could very well be her last because of him. Cal could spoil all her plans before she even got a chance to prove herself.

Annie stood up and began to pace, rehearsing in her mind what she'd say to the charity organizers when she called them—and more importantly what she'd do to Cal when she got her hands on him.

The front door opened, and she turned in anticipation, only to see Mrs. Batelle coming back into the house and disappearing down the hall.

Annie paced some more. Too much time had passed; it was becoming obvious that Cal wasn't going to make it. She finally gave herself over to her rage. She slammed her hand into her fist and let out an audible sigh. "Bastard!" she cursed quietly.

It didn't help. She sank back onto the sofa and thought about all the repercussions of this foul-up, her brain mentally clicking away in the manner of the cab meter—which was adding up. But its total would be nothing compared to the cost of missing the Florida event. That would probably cost her a job.

Then she heard the door open and close again, rapid footsteps and someone whistling. She raced to the parlor door in time to see Cal disappear up the stairs.

"Hi," he called casually over his shoulder. "Sorry I'm a little late. It'll just take me a minute to change—"

Annie was up the stairs behind him like a bullet. A mixture of relief and fury wrestled within her.

"Where the hell have you been?" she asked.

He continued upstairs without responding.

"The taxi's waiting, our flight's in just over an hour...."

"I know that," he said calmly. "Twenty minutes to shower and dress, thirty minutes to the airport, ten minutes to check in. It's under control, Annie."

She wasn't buying that, and when he disappeared into a bedroom, Annie barged in behind him. "You look awful. You need a shave. And you're wearing... you're wearing a tuxedo."

"Why, so I am," he answered, looking down in mock surprise.

"You've been to a party," she accused. "An all-night party."

Cal sat on the bed and took off his shoes and socks. "Why, Annie, you sound like a jealous wife. Yes, I've been to a party. It didn't last all night, but since it was in New York, I had to—"

"New York! You've been up there and back without telling me? I thought we agreed...no social events without my okay, especially in New York where the press is rapacious...."

Call stripped off his shirt. "It was a private party for old friends. Remember the rest of our agreement? My personal life is off-limits."

It took a moment for his last few words to register with Annie, who was mesmerized by the sight of a half-naked Cal Markam, newly cut hair tousled, ruddy face unshaven, bare chest muscular and bronzed.

While her eyes were absorbing his masculine charms, her brain somehow still managed to function. "Of course, your personal life is your own. If it doesn't conflict with your new image—and doesn't make the newspapers."

"No problem. The party was very private. My pal Rick's in New York, and a group of old friends—"

Annie snapped to attention. "Rick, your partner? Is this something involving Surfer Babes? Or women in bikinis? Was your good friend Charley there, too?" Annie was incensed. "The press will eat this up."

"First, Charley wasn't there. As far as I know, she's living in Europe now. Second, Rick's in New York on business, but I'm not involved. Third, there was no press at the party. So relax, Annie." He smiled at her with his eyes and at the same time reached for the zipper of his trousers. "I'm undressing now. Are you staying to watch?"

Annie turned her back. "I'm not watching, but I'm not leaving, either. I'm sticking with you, Cal, until the fund-raiser is over, sticking like glue."

She heard the sound of the zipper and then Cal hopping around, balancing on one foot as he pulled the trousers off and then standing a moment, in his underwear, she imagined, as if waiting for her to turn around.

When she didn't oblige, he padded barefoot across the floor.

"Suit yourself. You can join me in the shower if you want to. Plenty of room for two."

"Go ahead without me," she replied.

Cal smiled at her back and thought with pleasure that he'd detected another example of a sense of humor from Annie.

"We're running short of time," she reminded him.

"Don't worry." He stepped into the shower.

"There could be delays on the bridge or a stalled car, or . . ."

But the water was running loudly in the shower, and Cal didn't answer.

THEY BOARDED THE PLANE with only moments to spare. Annie was frantic. She was accustomed to arriving well in advance of flight time. But Cal seemed to enjoy their wild dash down the concourse to the plane.

She felt frazzled, hot and slightly out of control. He appeared fresh and relaxed in the clothes Annie had chosen for him. The flight attendants picked up on his cool and chatted with Cal as they served their beverages. They ignored Annie altogether.

"So, what's the schedule?" Cal asked after a sip of his drink. He was cleanly shaved, smelling of spicy after-shave, his eyes bright. He didn't seem like someone who had partied all night.

"I mailed you an agenda." Annie willed herself to adopt his state of relaxation. But she couldn't help noticing how the blue shirt brought out the deep tone of his azure eyes. Subconsciously, she must have had that in mind when she pulled it from his closet. Despite flying first-class, they were still intimately close in the airline seats. The experience was disconcerting, especially when her mind kept flashing back to the scene in his bedroom, to his bare chest and muscular arms.

She pushed the vision away. "Didn't you read it?" she asked, more sharply than necessary.

"Never had a chance, but I knew you'd bring another copy. You're real efficient that way." He flashed a smile. "Besides, I like the way you explain things."

Annie fished in her briefcase and handed Cal a folder. Obviously, she'd done as he expected and printed out several copies.

He opened his and studied their itinerary. "Okay," he said. "This looks simple enough. Arrive in Miami, transfer to a shuttle line to Mango Key." He looked over at her. "I've spent lots of great vacations in the Keys, fishing, snorkeling, sailing, lazing around."

"There'll be very little time for lazing on this day trip," she reminded him. "This is a chance—"

"To turn my image around," he finished for her. "I know." He returned to the schedule. "Proceed to Mango Key Nature Preserve where I make a large donation and give a speech about the plight of . . . Good Lord, is *this* what you've chosen to identify me with?"

"I told you we'd be sponsoring a very important endangered species."

"You never told me what it was. I specifically asked you—"

"How could I discuss anything with you? You were too busy partying in New York to even care. The crocodile protectors were anxious for a sponsor, and it seemed a good match. At this late date, our choices were pretty limited."

Cal looked at her, amazement etched in his expression. "Alligators? Don't tell me that's the best you could do—alligators."

"They're not alligators," Annie reprimanded quietly, aware that the passengers around them were listening to their argument. "They're crocodiles—narrower snouts, a different color—and they're endangered."

"So, I'm told, are the Florida panther, the black bear and the bobcat. And at least those have some kind of appeal. But alligators . . ." He shook his head in disgust. "I don't think I have it in me to make a speech about alligators."

Annie bristled as she thought of all the hours she'd put into setting up this appearance. "Listen to me, Cal Markam, it's not as if every environmental group in the country is dying for your support. The panther and black bear were already taken. I was lucky to get you anything. Remember, at this early stage in your makeover, you aren't that easy to sell."

Cal wasn't impressed. "This is what we're paying you the big bucks for—a trip to Florida to talk about alligators?"

"Crocodiles!"

She startled the flight attendant, who was about to take Cal's empty glass.

"Don't worry," Cal assured her. "My assistant here is a little excitable."

Annie shot him a dirty look but did lower her voice slightly. "Crocodiles are important to the whole ecological system of the Keys, and more than two hundred people are waiting for you to add your support to their cause. They expect an uplifting speech."

"And a big check, I've no doubt."

"I told you up front about the need to donate."

"I'm not complaining, only commenting. As for the speech, I assume you've written it."

"Of course. Since I had the feeling you might not get around to it. It's at the back of your folder."

Cal didn't bother to look.

Only hours away from the big event at the Nature Preserve and he was playing it cool, too cool for Annie. Cal was a loose cannon, an unknown entity. She had no idea what he would do next. "If you aren't interested in this event, I understand the Society for the Preservation of the Key Largo Wood Rat needs a benefactor, too. That might better fit your image."

Cal laughed. "So you do have a sense of humor, Annie Valentine, but I still don't think much of your choice. However, since you've booked me for the event, I'll make the speech." He pulled it from the file, took out a pen and began to make revisions.

Annie stifled a groan, closed her eyes and composed another speech—the one she'd make to Bert Canelli tomorrow when J.C. fired her.

GNATS BUZZED AROUND Annie's face as she stood a little apart from the crowd in the Mango Key Nature Preserve. She swatted at the insects but focused her attention on Cal, mesmerized like everyone else.

The man was a spellbinder, Annie conceded, a chameleon who seemed to change from careless playboy to serious, concerned citizen in front of her eyes. Instead of merely repeating her words, he'd added his own experiences to the speech, recalling his childhood vacations in the Keys and the beginnings of his ecological concern.

"Crocodiles are as old as the dinosaurs—they existed millions of years before humans, and yet we, the newcomers, seem determined to make their habitat unlivable by our carelessness and selfishness. We can't afford that, for each time we destroy a part of nature, we damage a part of ourselves."

That line was written by Annie but Cal spoke with such fervor, she would have sworn he'd written it himself.

He paused dramatically. The crowd was eager, hanging on his words with reverence and excitement. "This special place must remain for eternity as pure as the day it was created. And though I am only one concerned individual, I promise to do all within my power to make sure that happens."

As the applause swelled, Cal reached into his pocket for a check which he presented to the Save Our Crocs chairman. Cameras flashed, TV camcorders whirred, reporters and guests pushed forward. Cal was swallowed by the crowd.

MUCH LATER, as Annie listened to one of the enthusiastic SOC members rave about Cal, she couldn't resist a surge of pride. The society got more than they'd hoped for—and his donation to the cause was twice what Annie had expected.

She was also pleased with the way the press interviews had gone. Most of the reporters were feature writers, looking for angles for a full-page spread accompanied by lots of pictures. Cal cooperated with every photo request, posing again and again, his smile never wavering.

TV crews were on hand, too. With Cal's charisma and good looks Annie was sure that coverage on local Florida TV stations would turn up as clips on the national morning talk shows, exactly what she'd been hoping for.

Unfortunately, a couple of hard news reporters showed up, with not-so-subtle references to his reputation and cynical questions about Cal's sudden love of crocodiles. But to Annie's relief, no one asked about the paternity suits, and Cal managed to steer the topic back to the Nature Preserve and his love of the outdoors. It was difficult for even the most hardened reporter to criticize a man who'd just donated a bundle to a worthy cause—no matter what his motivation.

Cal had even toured the preserve, exploring the deep reaches of the crocodile habitat, studying the breeding ponds, showing concern over an injured croc and smiling at a nest of young ones. Very macho...yet very sensitive.

But where was he now? Annie glanced at her watch. If they were to keep to her schedule, they'd have to leave immediately. She extracted herself from the SOC enthusiast, smiling her thanks, and moved around the crowd, which had thinned considerably.

Cal was nowhere to be seen.

Trying not to show outward concern, she walked across the clearing, smiling, stopping to acknowledge compliments about her "boss," all the while keeping an eye out for Cal.

After half an hour of searching, including retracing the steps of their tour, Annie sank down on a bench by one of the lily ponds and looked across the bridge to the clearing. Even the stragglers were heading toward their cars, and the workmen had begun to disassemble the stage and remove the folding chairs.

Where the hell was Cal, and what the hell was he doing?

A crocodile swam by with what Annie considered a surly look. While she didn't want to have any bad thoughts about crocodiles—or about Cal—today of all days, she wished the reptile would disappear and Cal would reappear. Not necessarily in the same place, but if he didn't show up soon, the crocs could have him.

Moments later, Annie saw him strolling unhurriedly toward the bridge. She was on her feet instantly, charging toward him.

"Where were you? I've been waiting—"

"I do believe you missed me, Annie." Grinning broadly, Cal met her halfway across the bridge, grabbed her around the waist, lifted her high and whirled her around. "What a great day, huh? Couldn't have turned out better."

Annie clung to Cal while blue sky, green palms and white clouds careened crazily above her head. "Put me . . . put me . . . Thank you," she managed when he set her on her feet.

Cal took her arm and steered her back to the bench. "Sorry for the long wait, but I got caught by a reporter."

"Oh, no. Who? I thought they had all left."

"Worried that I might have blown it, Annie?"

"Well . . ."

"Despite your concerns, that won't happen." He looked her right in the eye and added seriously, "I always get what I want and I want to be the Markam CEO. So I performed admirably—for a female member of the press corps who had a few more questions."

Annie wrinkled her forehead. "The pretty brunette from the local radio station? I noticed how she kept hanging around."

"Yep, it was the brunette. In the short skirt. She was very persistent, and who am I to disappoint a lady?"

Annie rolled her eyes. "But where were you? I looked all over—"

Cal grinned. "You're sounding like a jealous wife again, Annie. The interview was in the parking lot at her news van. So don't worry, I handled myself like a gentleman, a concerned citizen, and a serious spokesman. My new agenda, right?"

Annie relaxed. "Right. There's only one little glitch. Because of that last interview, we missed the shuttle to Miami."

Cal didn't look at all concerned.

"So, I'll have to revise the schedule." She referred to her notes. "We can rent a car—"

"Or not," he interrupted.

"How else will we get to Miami? There are no more shuttles today, and we have to catch a flight from Miami to Philadelphia tonight." She looked at her watch. "We won't make the next one, but there are a couple of others before midnight, and—"

"Annie, Annie, stop and listen to me. The hard part is over. I performed well, don't you think?"

"Absolutely."

"Then let's celebrate by staying here tonight."

"Here?"

Cal laughed. "Not with the crocodiles. But I know a little inn—"

"Cal . . ."

"Listen to me, Annie. The drive to Miami is long and boring, and we'd probably have to hang around the airport for hours waiting for a flight."

She looked at him suspiciously. "You didn't plan this, did you, Cal?"

"Why, Annie, what a thing to say. Would you have wanted me to refuse an interview?"

"No, of course not, but your lateness is beginning to be a habit."

"In this case, easily remedied by enjoying an evening in the Keys and catching a shuttle in the morning. Why not?"

"Because . . ."

"I'm waiting."

"Because..." Surely there was a reason they couldn't stay. "We don't have any clothes."

Cal burst into laughter. "A real problem."

"Well, it is, Cal. Besides, we'd need toothbrushes, shampoo . . ."

"There are stores in the Keys, Annie. We might even buy T-shirts, sandals and shorts. Not a big expense for such a successful combination as Cal Markam and his 'assistant,' Annie Valentine. And we were a success, Annie."

"Well, yes, but . . ."

"Don't you think we deserve a treat? Sure we do," he answered for her. "Think about it. What's on the agenda tomorrow that you'll miss?"

"Phone calls. I have so many calls to make—"

"Not only are there stores in the Keys, there are also telephones. You'll be able to make all your calls from the Mango Inn. Come on, Annie, it'll be good for you." Cal looked around at the beauty of the Preserve. "It's restful here in the Keys. It's the perfect place to get to know each other, clear the air of any tension that's left between us. If we have to work together, we might as well be friends. Why not start here?"

Annie couldn't muster up any more arguments. "I guess we could talk about the next phases of the campaign. And it would be more relaxing . . ."

The croc surfaced very nearby and seemed to look right at her. "But as you say, not here . . ."

Cal took her hand. "What's the matter, Annie, not fond of our crocodile friend?"

Annie looked at the huge reptile. "I'm all for preserving him, but I don't want to spend the night with him."

Cal leaned close, his breath warm against her ear. "Then spend it with me."

AFTER DINNER on the veranda of the Mango Inn, Annie relaxed in a big white wicker chair beside Cal and thought about how easily she had acquiesced to his invitation to keep him company for the night. But, she told herself, it was less the innuendo of his words than their plain good sense that had convinced her. Why drive and wait when they could rest and enjoy the glorious setting? She inhaled the October air, heavy with the scent of the salty sea and the sweet tropical flowers that grew just beyond the veranda's wrought iron fence.

Dressed casually in the T-shirt, shorts and sandals she had bought at Cal's insistence, Annie had rarely felt more at ease. She drew a deep breath, relishing the moment.

"Nice, huh?" Cal asked.

"Yes, it is," she replied.

He hadn't been wrong about Annie, Cal decided. She really could enjoy herself in the right setting. And this was definitely it. They'd had dinner by candlelight in a secluded alcove beneath the veranda's overhanging red-tiled roof. He had enjoyed every moment of the meal, starting with the local conch chowder and grilled grouper and ending with the mandatory Key lime pie.

Annie had eaten with gusto, which pleased Cal, and she'd drunk the sweet, refreshing wine enthusiastically, going beyond what he suspected was her one glass limit. But he hadn't made a comment about it. He liked the idea that she was loosening up. Finally.

The dishes had been cleared from the table, a bottle of wine and two glasses left behind, and they were alone. He settled back into the comfortable chintz-covered cushions and smiled as he looked over at Annie.

"More wine?"

Annie shook her head as a burst of laughter made its way to them from around the corner of the patio.

"I've already had too much wine, but I'm enjoying myself, and it sounds like everyone else is, too."

"They're probably sports fishermen who've had a good day on the boat. Most people come down here to dive or fish. The more laid-back you become, the better. And you fit in perfectly, wearing those shorts and T-shirt." He let his gaze wander up her body. "I was right about your great legs," he added with a grin.

Annie managed to control a blush. "I never would have thought of dressing like this for dinner," she said.

"Annie, we're in the Keys, remember?"

"I don't know anything about the Keys," she answered honestly, "or Florida, for that matter. This is my first trip."

Cal put down his wineglass and looked at her in astonishment. "You've never been to Florida? Not even on spring break? I thought every college kid east of the Mississippi made it to Florida at least once."

"Not *every* kid. Some of us had to work." She tried to keep the defensiveness out of her voice as she thought of the different ways she and Cal had grown up. She imagined he had spent most of his holidays lolling on the beach in some exotic location. Annie studied his face for signs of pity. Instead, he seemed merely curious.

"You worked during all your school vacations?"

Annie nodded, reluctant to explain more, but Cal was persistent.

"Even Christmas?"

"Especially Christmas. That was the busy time at the drugstore in my hometown."

"So, when you went home for the holidays you filled in at the local store. Pretty industrious," he commented.

"Actually, I started working there when I was thirteen. I—" Annie broke off. "Let's talk about something else."

"Like your make-over campaign for me?"

"Well, I do have some more ideas—"

Cal broke into laughter. "Why don't we skip the remaking of Cal Markam for one night and talk about the life and times of Annie Valentine? I want to hear about the real Annie, starting with the little girl who worked in a drugstore."

"I wasn't that interesting," she demurred.

"You are now." Cal reached for her hand and held it tight. "And I bet you were then. But let me decide about that." He looked straight into her eyes. "If we're going to work together, we should know all about each other. It'll be good for our business relationship. God knows you have all the facts about me. So, it's your turn."

Cal's hand was warm and firm on hers, exerting just enough pressure to keep her from pulling away without effort. Annie decided not to make the effort. She liked the contact. It seemed to suit the mood of the evening.

"Where do I begin?" she asked.

"With the thirteen-year-old. No—" he decided. "With your parents."

"My dad still lives in the town where I grew up. My mom died when I was twelve."

Cal squeezed her hand. "That must have been hard on you," he said softly.

For a moment Annie felt tears sting her eyes. Memories of her mother together with such empathy from Cal made her momentarily vulnerable. But Annie didn't like being vulnerable. She blinked back the tears and continued her story.

"My dad works in a steel mill near Pittsburgh. There aren't many jobs back there now, but that life has never been easy, and he's used to it, I guess. He's gotten laid off in bad times, but he always stayed there, and he always got hired back. I guess after thirty years, he's a survivor. Anyway, it's all he knows, and he's good at his job. Some people might not consider that much of an accomplishment, being a blue-collar worker all your life—"

Cal caught a rebuke in her words and took his hand away. "Any job that a man—or woman—likes is important. I'm not a snob, Annie, no matter what you think." She was very defensive, this Annie Valentine, Cal realized. She reacted to criticism when none was implied. "Your father sounds like a proud man and a hardworking one."

"He is."

"You got your grit from him. That's easy to see."

"I guess I did. There wasn't much choice in the town where we lived."

"Which was called—"

"Milltown. Pretty original, isn't it?"

Cal laughed. "Tell me about growing up in Milltown."

"Not much to tell," she replied ruefully. "I went to school and worked to save money for university. Dad paid my tuition, but he couldn't do everything. I made enough to take care of books, food and clothes, and I got a loan that took care of my other expenses."

"I bet you got some scholarship money, too."

She looked up at him quizzically. "How did you know that?"

"Easy. You're very bright, and you have your dad's grit. Even though it wasn't exactly my choice, I'm glad to have you on my side, Annie Valentine."

Cal felt a surge of pleasure at the look on her face, an almost childlike flush of joy. Yes, she was a very interesting woman, he decided, and more complex than she seemed.

"You told me you worked in Harrisburg."

"I was a kind of gofer for a small PR firm, but it was a start. Gradually, I worked my way up and took on more important clients. I handled a major retail store that managed to thrive during a down economy. I guess people began to take notice of me."

"I don't blame them."

"Anyway, just as it seemed like time for me to move on, I got a call from Bert Canelli in Philadelphia. Let's just say that he made me an offer I couldn't refuse."

Cal looked at her over the rim of his wineglass. "And you left your boyfriend behind?"

"How did you—I mean, what makes you think that?"

He shrugged. "Just intuitive. About women." His expression didn't change, but Annie saw a glint in his eyes. "You're young and attractive, so it figures you'd have some guy crazy about you. Maybe a lot of guys back in Harrisburg."

This was getting too personal, Annie thought. She was glad they were no longer touching. She fiddled with her napkin while Cal waited. Finally, she raised her eyes to his. "Just one. My college sweetheart. We moved to Harrisburg and lived together for a while."

"What happened?" He was seriously interested, not just curious anymore.

"My job, I guess. Everything was great at first, but the more time I spent at work the more he resented it. He was doing well in his career, and he thought that should be enough for me, too. He didn't understand how important it is for me to succeed on my own. I don't want to let down my Dad—or anyone else who believes in me. I guess I have a lot to prove," she added with a burst of honesty.

"If he didn't understand that, he wasn't right for you."

Annie looked at Cal wonderingly. "How do we ever know that, do you suppose? Hit and miss? Trial and error?"

"You're asking the wrong person," he told her.

"Well, anyway, it doesn't matter now. I have a new job, a new apartment and a new project. Everything I need."

Cal decided not to tackle the subject of Annie's needs, not now, when they seemed to be moving toward a tentative kind of relationship. But he couldn't resist one more question. "Did you and your ex-boyfriend ever argue?"

Annie was thoughtful for a moment. "Nope, it wasn't that we argued, more that we just didn't talk. Especially at the end. It was as if we had nothing left to talk about, let alone argue over."

"Not like us."

"No," she said with a wry grin. "You and I can always argue."

"And talk." He looked at his watch. "A couple of hours' worth of talk." Suddenly it was important to Cal that everything be all right between them. He thought about the way their day had begun and grimaced inwardly.

"Listen," he began. "About those alliga— I mean crocodiles. I overreacted. Your idea was great, and I apologize. I guess you took me by surprise. I'll have to remember that about you. The surprising Ms. Valentine," he teased.

"From now on I'll keep you more informed." She was still serious.

"And I'll pay more attention," he vowed.

"While we're clearing the air, I'm sorry I overreacted in Philadelphia this morning," she told him. "It's just that I have a thing about time."

Cal chuckled. "Yeah, so do I—I'm perpetually late. I'll try to be on time—"

"And I'll try not to jump to conclusions about your activities."

Cal held out his hand. "Truce?" Annie took it, and he realized how much he liked holding hands with her. This time he wasn't going to let go.

"Truce," she repeated softly.

"Good. Now how about another glass of wine?"

"Oh, no," Annie said quickly. "I've had enough."

The group of fishermen on the far side of the veranda left noisily, walking past them, laughing. Then everything was very still and quiet with only the tinkling of a piano wafting across the night from the bar.

"Time to dance," Cal suggested.

"Dance? Here? There's no one—"

He got to his feet and pulled Annie up. "That's right. There's no one dancing. In fact there's no one here but us. So, why not?"

"I really—I don't—" Annie held back.

"You don't know how to dance?"

"Of course, I do. It's just that I haven't danced in a long time."

"Don't worry, it's just like riding a bicycle. Let me remind you."

He took her in his arms.

4

CAL MOVED SLOWLY, crossing the patio in time to the
soft music of the piano, holding her close. The uneven
stones made for bumpy dancing, but he managed to
avoid the worst of them and maneuver Annie to a space
outside the restaurant window where the footing was
smoother.

Annie tried to joke. "Not only do I have to learn all
over again, I don't even have the benefit of a dance
floor."

"I better remind you that there are people dancing
inside. They might see you step on my toes," he chal-
lenged. "Wouldn't that be worse than dancing on these
rocks?"

She wasn't so sure. If they moved inside, at least she
wouldn't be alone with him in the night breeze, close,
too close, with his arm firmly around her waist.

The music wasn't so far away now. Through the
window they could hear the crisp, clear notes of the piano, a familiar soft and dreamy tune, something from
an old movie, Annie thought. The title hovered just
outside her memory, but she knew why it was so elu-
sive. Anything would be at this moment, with Cal's
arm pressed against the small of her back, pulling her
so she molded into him, her breasts against his solid

chest, her stomach, pelvis, thighs hugging his. She tried
to move away a bit, but he stopped her.

"Relax, Annie. Lean against me and relax—and you
won't step on my toes."

But she couldn't relax. She was tense, resistant.
Maybe if she closed her eyes and tried to give herself to
the music as he seemed to do so easily...

She gave it a try, listening to his steady breathing and
feeling the slow, even beat of his heart, hoping to du-
plicate it. Impossible, she thought. Impossible to force
her heart to slow down. It felt as if it were pounding out
of her chest.

He didn't seem to notice. "Now, isn't this just like
riding a bicycle all over?" he whispered against her ear.

"Not really, I—"

"Let me show you." He stepped backward and she
followed. Then to the side. She moved with him. His
rhythm was so easy, his movements so elegant, so
practised and sure, that even a rusty dancer could follow.

Slowly, she grew accustomed to the feeling of being
in his arms, accustomed to the sway of his body. And
the last traces of her anxiety melted away. She rested
one hand comfortably against the strong muscles of his
shoulder, and adjusted her other hand, which he'd en-
folded possessively within his. It felt so right. There was
certainly no reason not to end the evening with a dance,
no reason not to enjoy herself before getting back into
the work mode. After all, Annie really hadn't danced
since college. Why not get into it for just a few minutes?

But maybe this was the wrong kind of enjoyment, she told herself suddenly. If she kept her eyes closed, she might indulge too much in this magical moment. And that wouldn't be such a good idea. Annie forced her eyes open.

That was not a good idea, either, because of what she found directly in her view. She was looking at the smooth skin of Cal's muscular neck. She concentrated on the three blue buttons of his polo shirt and avoided looking at him.

But again, Cal managed to thwart her plan as he stepped away a little, causing her to look up. He was shaking his head thoughtfully. "Out of all the gin joints in all the world, you had to walk into this one."

Annie frowned.

"What's the matter, don't you like my Bogie imitation?"

She was truly puzzled.

"Annie, I was doing Humphrey Bogart in *Casablanca*. I thought my timing was perfect since the guy at the piano was playing 'As Time Goes By.'"

"Oh, that's the song! I thought it sounded familiar."

"Only familiar? One of the most famous love songs of all time? Obviously, you're not a true romantic like me."

"A true romantic?" Annie retorted. "That's not what I'd call you."

"That's because the only Cal Markam you've really seen is the one in the press. Tonight you're getting to know the real me, the romantic Cal Markam."

"That's not part of my job description," she said.

"If you're going to change me, you have to know all my facets."

Suddenly the pianist switched tempo, into something fast and jazzy. Without any warning, Cal whirled her around, across the patio, over the bumpy stones, around and around, with Annie following him every step of the way—laughing joyfully—until the song ended. Then he went into an old-fashioned dip, bending her backward over his arm until her hair swept the stone patio.

He leaned over her, his lips just a millimeter from hers, and Annie struggled to right herself. But again he was in control.

Annie twisted around, grabbing at his waist with both hands, forcing him to pull her upright rather than let her fall. Still holding on to him, she managed to stand firmly on both feet. "That was some ending," she said, trying to make light of it.

"See, it all comes back, just like riding a bicycle. You need to learn to trust me, Annie," he teased.

She straightened her T-shirt and tugged at her shorts, trying to put herself back in order. Then she stood upright and declared, "And you need to trust me. After all, I'm the one in charge of the new Cal." She ran her fingers through her tousled hair and finally managed to catch her breath.

Cal held up his hand. "Enough work talk—"

"We haven't had *any* work talk—"

"Exactly. Let's keep it that way," he teased. "As soon as you catch your breath there's something I want to show you."

She looked around. "What?"

"It's not here. It's out there." He pointed across the wrought iron fence into the blackness. "I took a walk before dinner and found a white sand beach. It's just a tiny crescent, but it's perfect. I want to show you the ocean by moonlight from that beach."

"Oh, no." This time Annie held up her hand. Dancing with Cal on the patio at the Mango Inn had pushed the bounds of their professional relationship. Traipsing off into the night with her client was something else again.

"Why not?"

"Because . . ."

"Once more, you're left without an excuse, Annie. It's your first trip to Florida. All you've seen so far is the Nature Preserve and the Mango Inn. You haven't even seen the ocean—"

"I saw the ocean when we checked in."

"—by moonlight," he finished.

After a long, thoughtful pause, Annie gave herself over to the real feelings that possessed her. In fact, she didn't want to work; she wanted to walk along the shoreline and feel the ocean at her feet and the wind in her face. Just for a little while.

"Okay," she said. "For a few minutes."

Cal took her hand and led her across the patio, through the wrought iron gate and along the wide stone steps. A path of crushed shells wound downward to the tiny jewel of a beach. Beyond the white crescent, the ocean gleamed silvery in the moonlight.

"There are no waves," she said.

"No, the reef from Miami to Key West creates a bay here," he explained. "Not exactly a surfer's paradise. But it's perfect for lovers."

Annie ignored that remark as she followed his lead and slipped off her sandals to walk in the sand. They reached the waterline, and Annie discovered that the ocean was warm and caressing, like liquid silk against her skin.

"I can't believe that the water's so warm," she said. "October seems like summer here."

"Endless summer. That's also what I liked about California. The climate, the sun, the warmth."

They walked along, splashing in the ocean, free and easy. The moonlight seemed to spill right down on them, and when Annie looked over at Cal, he was illuminated. She was struck again by what a handsome man he was. The planes of his face were strong and chiseled, the muscles of his shoulders hard and bronzed. He moved like an Adonis on long, well-muscled legs. He was in his element, a man who knew how to enjoy himself.

"I wonder how you're going to adjust," she said suddenly, "when you've gotten used to California weather and suddenly have to trade that climate for Philadelphia where the winters are dreadful."

"Oh, but Annie, remember. I grew up in Philadelphia, so the climate's no big surprise. Don't worry. I'm not about to cut and run. You must know that, since I've just made a speech about one of my least favorite subjects, the crocodile. I can give up California—I can give up anything—to get my hands on Markam Investments. That's my goal, but that doesn't mean I'm not going to enjoy myself on the way."

"Have you always been determined to have fun no matter what?"

He shrugged. "I guess so. I don't spend time analyzing myself."

Annie couldn't help being curious. "Were you a rebellious kid?"

"The usual. Broken curfews, sneaking out after my parents were asleep." He laughed. "My bedroom was on the second floor, but there was a convenient tree next to the window. I made it through high school and promised my folks I'd finish university, and I did, without a major scandal." He chuckled. "Course, there were a few minor ones along the way."

"Then California."

"Yep. I was totally independent and free to indulge myself, to let go until the time came when I had to get serious again." He gave her hand a squeeze. "But all this Cal Markam talk is boring on a moonlit night." He guided her toward a small spit of land that curved out into the sea. "Come on, there's something else I have to show you."

She followed, enjoying the feel of her bare feet in the sugary sand.

"It's still here," he said, pulling her along toward a cluster of palm trees. Strung between two of them was a huge rope hammock. "I bet this is a great place to relax."

When she realized his intention, Annie tried to dig her feet into the sand. But Cal was in control, his grip firm on her hand, and before she could protest, he'd flopped into the hammock and pulled her down beside him. Despite her misgivings, she laughed with joy as they swung in the hammock, legs dangling over the side, feet skimming the sand.

Cal gave a push with his foot, and the hammock swung higher. He fell backward against the roped webbing. "Lean back and look up at the moon and the stars. There must be a million of them. You can't see them in the city because of all the illuminated skyscrapers, but out here there's not anything but sky."

Without lying back, Annie looked up at the sky and saw that what he said was true. The blackness was crowded with stars, blinking magically.

Cal gave another push, and the hammock rocked crazily. Annie grabbed for a handhold, but momentum was the victor, and she tumbled back against Cal.

His arms closed around her. "Gotcha," he said.

She struggled to sit upright in spite of the erratic movement of the hammock. But her efforts only put her even more off balance. She was flung against Cal, her body pressed close to his. She looked up and found him laughing down at her, his face only inches away. She couldn't help but join in his laughter.

"You're a great-looking woman, Annie, especially when you laugh. Your eyes dance when you laugh." He kissed her cheek in a way that was so natural she didn't even think to protest. "And the moonlight does all kinds of wonderful things to your hair." He ran his fingers through the short tendrils, still looking deeply into her eyes. Then he moved his hand downward to cup her chin. "This calls for a real kiss."

His lips were warm, soft, enveloping—not demanding. He kissed with a gentle curiosity, exploring her mouth easily, sensuously. Even though he'd told Annie he was going to kiss her, she wasn't prepared. Not for Cal's mouth on hers, and certainly not for her reaction.

Instinctively, she closed her eyes and gave herself to the kiss. She knew what she was doing, and yet she didn't know. The moment simply took hold of her, and the moment was all. She heard his soft sigh of pleasure as she settled into the kiss and into his arms. It all just happened; it all seemed so right.

"Oh, yes, Annie, this was a great idea." His breath was warm against her ear, and then his tongue touched the outer rim, before tasting the smooth inner surface. She trembled against him, giving little gasps of delight. She was strangely light-headed, lost in the pleasure he evoked.

Cal's hands were working their own magic. She felt his fingers under her T-shirt, caressing the bare flesh of her back, drifting along her spine. His touch was hypnotic. It was as if he'd put her in a trance. In the back of her mind, Annie realized she was falling under his spell, knew she should try to break it.

But she couldn't. His lips were on hers again; his tongue glided along her lips until with a little sigh she opened her mouth and felt his tongue touch hers. The sigh turned to a whimper of pleasure. Her nipples tingled with need. She could feel them tighten and swell, pressed hard against him. Deep inside, in the secret recesses of her body, a slow throbbing ache began to build.

His hair was crisp and damp beneath her fingers, his leg between hers was hard and muscular. She was surrounded by Cal, captured. Yes, the thought nagged at the back of her again, she was captured.

Then he spoke softly to her, pushing the thought away. "You are some kind of kisser, Annie. Just as I thought, full of surprises."

She looked at him through a haze of passion. His eyes were dark with desire, his hair tousled, his mouth curved in a satisfied grin. Annie's heart was pounding so hard she didn't even try to respond.

How had this happened? How had she gotten into the hammock with Cal, lain back beside him, become entwined with him, kissed him and enjoyed it? Everything had begun with that dangerous decision to take a moonlight stroll along the beach with Cal Markam. The rest had been orchestrated by him.

Annie gave a little moan.

Cal laughed. "I hope that's a sound of pleasure, not despair." He kissed her again, fully, expertly, his tongue grazing hers, his lips firm, warm, seeking. Then he broke off the kiss and wrapped her completely in his arms, keeping their bodies tightly entwined. She could feel the hard strength of his erection pushing against her. She couldn't move away from it, and somehow she didn't want to.

Cal's tone was low and seductive. "We can go to my room, Annie . . ."

He allowed the suggestion to sink in, waited for a response that didn't come. She couldn't form the words of protest that her mind told her to voice.

"Or we can make love here. Wouldn't that be a great choice? To make love under the stars, listening to the sea." His mouth was on hers again, and he moved his hands along her spine, over her shoulder blade, then slid them beneath her T-shirt toward her breasts.

Annie's head was spinning, her senses overloaded. His kisses made her lose all sense of right or wrong, of decorum or responsibility. The thought of making love to him, of lying naked in his arms, of taking him inside her waiting body, made her weak with desire.

But she couldn't ignore the thought nagging at her mind. She was under a spell, and that spell would end after she slept with Cal. They'd have a wonderful night of pleasure, and the next morning she'd be just another of Cal Markam's long line of lovers. And she was sure Cal wouldn't let her forget what went on between them; he'd make innuendos, tease her and undermine what little authority she had with him. Their business relationship would be shattered, and so would her career.

Unaware of her thoughts, Cal continued to stroke and kiss her, murmuring softly, "Oh, Annie, I want you so much it makes me ache all over."

Annie wondered how many times he had whispered those words, how many lovers had been seduced by those words, and how many women he had made love to and then dropped from his life.

Annie drew deeply on the last vestiges of her self-respect and integrity, dug her feet into the sand, gave a sudden push, and responded in what she hoped was a clear, determined voice, "No, Cal, I don't think—"

But her attempt to rise caused the hammock to swing wildly, and when Cal tried to sit up and stop the motion, the hammock rocked and they both flipped over the edge.

"What the hell—" was all Cal managed before they hit the sand with a thud. Annie landed on top of him in a tangle of arms and legs. Startled, she was unhurt, but underneath her Cal didn't look so good. His eyes were closed, and she suspected the fall had knocked the wind out of him.

"Cal," she said tentatively, touching his cheek.

He opened one eye and gazed coolly at her. "I believe I got the message, Annie. You're saying no to romance."

Annie struggled to her knees with as much grace as she could muster. "Are you all right?"

He pushed up on one elbow. "Nothing that a cold shower won't cure," he replied curtly.

Annie backed away on her hands and knees through the sand, and when she was clear of him she stood up and moved toward the path. "I'll go to my room now. It's late, and our flight leaves at nine in the morning."

Cal got to his feet. "See you then."

With those three words ringing in her ears, Annie fled along the beach, berating herself furiously. She'd made a real mess of things by not leaving after their last dance. In fact, it hadn't been wise to dance with him in the first place. The next mistake was going to the beach with him. And the kiss. If they hadn't kissed, she never would have let it go any further.

She reached the end of the beach, found her sandals and slipped them on. She'd behaved unprofessionally, that's all there was to it. But he'd read more into the kiss than she'd meant him to. Now all the good feelings that had been building between them on the trip were gone.

As she started toward the inn, Annie heard a splash and turned around. In the moonlight, she could see Cal's head moving through the water as he swam, his arms slicing the waveless sea. The swim was obviously his version of a cold shower.

Annie groaned. She'd set up a perfect formula for disaster. A romantic location. A dangerous man. A foolish woman.

CAL WOKE UP in a rotten mood, and it stayed with him. He rode beside Annie to the Mango Key airstrip in virtual silence. The prop plane that flew them on the shuttle hop into Miami International was loud and bumpy, which didn't help the mood, but at least the flight was too noisy for them to talk, and Cal was grateful for that.

Now, settling into their seats for the trip back to Philadelphia, he was still moody and still avoiding too much contact with her. If they started communicating, they might end up rehashing the night before. He didn't want that, and he had no desire to talk about the next phase of his transformation, either.

Everything had gone well until the hammock. Dammit, he thought, everything had been perfect. His speech. The tasty dinner. The sensual dance. The romantic walk on the beach. Hell, if a moonlit night in the Florida Keys couldn't loosen the woman up, what could?

He opened his eyes and sneaked a look at her. In fact, she *had* shown another side out there on the beach, at least for a little while. Sure, she was still uptight and tense, eager to succeed, sitting there looking busy and officious as she checked off items on a list with her pen.

But she wasn't all business. They both knew that now. She had a passionate, sexy side and was very much a temptress when she wanted to be. Last night, for a few delicious moments, she'd wanted to go wild. She'd wanted it like crazy.

He briefly watched her work then closed his eyes. Now it was business as usual, and when it came to business, they had very different ideas. In the past, he'd had what he considered warm and personal relationships with a couple of the women who worked for him. When the affairs ended, they'd remained friends and continued to work together. Business and pleasure had mixed very well.

"So what's the big deal?" he muttered.

"Excuse me?" Annie replied. "Big deal about what?"

Cal hesitated. He and Annie were on different wavelengths—nope, he decided, different planets—when it came to sexual relationships. And everything else, it seemed. He decided there was no point in pursuing his argument.

"So, what's the next big deal you're cooking up?"

"I was just going over my—I mean our—plans. We're going to get involved in Philadelphia's cultural side."

"Oh, are we?"

"Yes, you know, opera, ballet, museums. Photo opportunities for the society page and at just the right time of year. I hear this is the beginning of the social season."

Cal groaned. "Well, you hear right. Take it from someone who knows. I've lived through too many Philadelphia social seasons. And quite frankly, I wonder if I can bear another one."

"You'll bear this one," Annie assured him.

"It's boring, Annie. So boring you won't believe it."

"Boring doesn't matter. Our goal matters. Good PR for you and a new image. We don't need to worry about having fun along the way."

Cal shook his head. "That's exactly what we *do* need to worry about. Let me put it this way. We're both headed for the same destination, Annie, but the difference between us—or one of the differences—is that you don't care about anything but the destination. I want to enjoy the journey."

"Well, I suppose it's possible to do both."

"Course it is. So let's just relax and start enjoying ourselves—now." He reached for her hand just as a baby's piercing cry rang out at the entrance of the plane.

Cal jolted upright. "She'd better not be bringing that kid this way," he said.

A young woman struggled down the aisle toward them hauling a diaper bag, baby carrier—and squirming baby. "Oh, no," he murmured. He looked around quickly and saw the empty seat across the aisle. "Here she comes, and guess where she's going to sit?"

"Maybe not," Annie ventured, glancing at Cal. But he was right. The woman was making a beeline for the aisle seat across from Cal.

"I'll trade places with you," Annie offered, puzzled and slightly annoyed by his reaction.

"What difference will eighteen inches make, Annie? I don't want the baby near me."

That did it for Annie; the placating was over. "Babies have as much right to fly as anyone else," she berated.

As the young mother struggled with her bags, a man in the seat behind her got up to help. Cal didn't budge. And the baby kept on crying.

"As soon as they get settled, everything'll be okay," Annie said firmly, just as the baby let out another wail.

Cal raised a quizzical eyebrow. "That's what you call okay?"

"What is it with you and children?" Annie demanded. "First you refuse to do PR with kids, and now you're overreacting to that poor little baby." She lowered her voice. "Is it the paternity suits? Is that it?"

Cal sighed. "Not that again. No, it isn't the paternity suits, though obviously they didn't help my attitude." He shrugged. "The truth is, I've never been around babies. I don't know anything about them, have no idea how to deal with them."

"No nieces or nephews?"

"I'm an only child, and none of my friends have children yet."

"And you have a closed mind," Annie added.

"Let's just say babies aren't an important part of my life. They seem very limited in what they can do."

"But the things they can do are fascinating," Annie countered.

"Sure, they can spit up, wet their pants—and worse. And how about crying so hard no one can stop them?" He cocked his head toward the mother and baby.

"The baby'll be quiet once the plane takes off," she tried again.

"Or it might decide to cry the whole trip. I'm not going to sit around and wait to find out."

"Then what do you plan to do—have the baby thrown off the plane? Or maybe you'll get off yourself and charter a jet back to Philadelphia," Annie suggested.

"Not a bad idea, but I'll save it for the next trip. Meanwhile, my plan is a simple one—to get my seat changed. There has to be one empty seat on this whole damned flight that's not next to a kid, somewhere quiet and peaceful. I don't care if I'm in first class or not. I'll just ask the flight attendant."

"I can't believe you're going to make a big deal about sitting next to a crying child," she argued over the ear-splitting cries of the baby. "It's absurd."

He unbuckled his seat belt and stood up just as the infant let out another scream. Cal smiled knowingly at Annie and then leaned down, his face close to hers. "I don't have to listen to this baby cry all the way to Philadelphia. If you want to play the martyr role, be my guest. I'm finding another seat even if I have to pay someone to change with me."

Annie shrugged. "Go ahead. You always do what you want to, anyway."

"That's right, I do." He gave her a patronizing pat on the shoulder and disappeared down the aisle.

Moments later, a teenage boy outfitted with headphones and a portable stereo slid into the seat beside Annie, obviously pleased to be sitting in first class. Cal had made his deal; Cal had gotten his way. No big surprise about that, Annie thought.

It was just another example of their many differences, which Cal had pointed out himself. They never agreed about anything. They were always at each other's throats—or in each other's arms.

No more of that, she decided. If she couldn't control Cal or what he did, she could control the situations they were placed in. From now on, she'd make a point not to be alone with him, and she certainly wouldn't plan any overnight junkets. Day trips only. Of course, the trip to Mango Key hadn't been intended as an overnighter until Cal started making arrangements. He had manipulated her into spending the night and then seduced her into a walk on the beach.

He had a terrible reputation with women; he'd been involved in two paternity suits. Annie of all people should have thought about that. Her job was to change the public's conception of that reputation, but meanwhile she sure as hell had better not forget what he was really like.

The plane hit a pocket, and the baby, who'd almost fallen asleep, woke up with a vengeance.

And he doesn't even like babies, Annie thought. What kind of a man is that?

5

ANNIE STOOD in the middle of the well-dressed crowd at the party and pondered over her success. She had kept her vow. She hadn't been alone with Cal for nearly a month, and they were right on track, halfway through his image change. All her plans were going smoothly. Well, there had been one pretty serious slipup, she reminded herself. Serious enough that if Cal hadn't defended her so effectively, she'd have been in big trouble with Bert. No major damage had been done, though, so she preferred not to think about it.

Generally, she'd been successful and she attributed it partially to her skill at keeping Cal at arm's length. She arranged to meet Cal at each scheduled event or pick him up in the limo—as she'd done tonight for the ballet benefit—so that they were never alone. Every outing had been in Philadelphia or its environs; no more out-of-town trips, no more opportunities for intimate evenings together.

It was all for the best, Annie told herself as she made her way through the maze of people at the postperformance reception. It was being held in an enormous heated tent, decorated all in white with crystal chandeliers, floral centerpieces and, for an added touch, white swans swimming in a nearby fountain.

Cal was in his element. She saw him across acres of white tablecloths, surrounded by long-legged ballerinas who seemed to think everything he said was incredibly amusing. She'd come to realize that women flocked to Cal like bees to honey. He didn't really have to do anything; it just happened.

But so far, he hadn't gotten involved with anyone in Philadelphia, much to the dismay of the gossip columnists. They were salivating for Cal to find the woman of his dreams—or at least to embark on a hot affair. Cal continued to disappoint them with his stock retort: "I'm too busy beginning a new life in the city I love to find time for romance."

Annie doubted that.

He disappeared occasionally to New York or Boston or Stowe, Vermont. She was sure those trips were scheduled to visit the woman—or women—in his life. "Looking up old friends," he'd say vaguely. "Seeing some shows, skiing . . . you know, Annie, having fun." And since nothing appeared about his trips in the press, Annie merely nodded. As long as his private life stayed private, how could she object?

Cal didn't mention the scene in the hammock, and neither did she. That didn't mean she never thought about it. She did, often. In fact, she seemed to have Cal on her mind most of the time. Of course, that was partly because he was her A-number-one client, her ticket to a successful career. But no matter what she told herself, it was also because she remembered that night in the hammock, remembered what it was like to be in his arms, remembered what it was like to kiss him.

Annie stopped a passing waiter, whisked a glass of champagne from his tray and took a sip.

So, they'd never mentioned the Florida trip except to review the handful of favorable clippings it had garnered and congratulate each other. Perhaps they'd exchanged a few uncomfortable glances. But she didn't want to talk about their midnight encounter, and she appreciated his silence.

She liked that about him, along with a lot of other things. Week by week she learned more about Cal. He had a sharp temper, but it didn't bother her as much now as it once had. He didn't hold grudges. Obviously, he'd been angry at her over the hammock incident and their argument on the plane, but he hadn't dwelt on it. As soon as the anger was out of his system, it had been back to business as usual. She appreciated his attitude because she didn't want any interruptions in her plans. And it kept their relationship on a purely professional level.

Annie wandered to the buffet table and began to fill up a plate. She'd drunk half the champagne quickly and now was ravenously hungry. Pâté on top of salmon on top of cheeses. She piled them high and then tried to shove something onto a cracker. It wasn't working. She put down the plate and her champagne, then carefully spread a cracker. It was on the way to her mouth when she felt a touch on her bare shoulder.

"Hiding from me?"

Cal's hand was warm on her skin. "Just grabbing a bite—or trying to," she replied.

"You didn't have a chance to eat at home?" His hand was still resting on her shoulder.

Annie laughed. "Actually, the cupboards are bare. I never seem to have time to get to the market."

"So, you arrange these events based on the quality of the food served?"

"Absolutely. Didn't I do a good job tonight?" She bit into the pâté.

"The food's good. No doubt about that. But I've eaten my fill, Annie. And I've said everything I can about ballet. How much longer do we have to submit ourselves to this?"

"Until the photographer arrives. Then a few shots in the white tent with the beautiful ballerinas and their generous benefactor, and we can leave."

She was amazed to have gotten Cal here in the first place. The Community Ballet Foundation wasn't on the top of his list. In fact, ballet was right down there with opera, which he particularly disliked. But CBF was the kind of organization that would impress the Markam Board members, slightly highbrow and yet with a strong outreach program for young people. Thanks to a nice donation, Cal was now a trustee for the foundation. A little icing on the cake for his new image.

But that was also the rub. As such, he was obligated to attend opening-night performances—and linger awhile at the party afterward. Annie realized she could have lost him from boredom if it hadn't been for the beautiful ballerinas. They'd saved the day. Now all she had to do was hang on to Cal until the photo opportunities presented themselves.

Glancing up at him over her champagne, she knew how to keep his attention. "You seemed to be enjoying yourself a few minutes ago."

He bit. "You mean with the corps de ballet?"

"A lovely group of young women."

Cal nodded in agreement. "But I was just doing my job, Annie, making friends with the artists in an organization I support financially."

"And support it well," Annie added. But Cal wasn't listening. His attention was centered over her shoulder. Annie turned around.

"Trouble is on the way," Cal said. "In the form of my Aunt Dee. Watch out. She's wearing her barracuda smile." Before Annie had a chance to react, the woman had crossed to them. She was tall and slender, her dark hair pulled severely back from her face, her dress an elegant, sequined scarlet gown.

Annie had felt pretty good in her short black dress—until now. The vision in scarlet was designed to put every other woman in her place.

"Cal, darling! I had no idea you were a balletomane." She placed her lips an inch from his cheek and kissed the air dramatically.

"Aunt Dee, what a fantastic surprise," Cal said. "You've just made my evening."

Annie read the sarcasm in Cal's tone, but his aunt seemed oblivious to it. She was too busy checking out Annie. "I'm Delores Markam Frame, Cal's aunt, and you are—"

"Annie . . . Valenti." It took her only a split second to make the decision to lie. Dee Frame looked like the kind of woman who could—and would—track Annie Valentine back to Bert Canelli's firm in a split second. With a glass of champagne in one hand and a plate piled high with hors d'oeuvres in the other, shaking hands was out of the question. The two women stared at each other.

The smile on Dee's lips wasn't reflected in her cool blue eyes. "How charming to meet you."

Cal crossed his arms over his chest and watched the two of them in silence.

"How do you know my darling nephew?" Dee asked, then continued before Annie could respond. "I guess you're not a business associate?" She looked Annie up and down. "You don't look like the type. Not one of those surfer sweeties."

Annie bristled. Dee knew how to conceal a barb within a compliment. She decided not to honor it with a response.

Cal stepped in for her. "The term is Surfer Babe, Dee, and Annie's not one. Our relationship is much more personal."

Annie shot Cal a warning look which he ignored as he wrapped one arm proprietarily around her waist. "I tell you, Dee, there's nothing like the support of a good woman to turn a man's life around."

"Hmm," Dee said thoughtfully. "I must admit your image is changing, Cal. I've noticed your photos in the paper quite a bit recently—the museum gala, the botanical gardens benefit.... I find the new Cal Markam quite fascinating. This metamorphosis wouldn't have anything to do with your father's retirement, would it, Cal?"

"What you see before you is a new man, Dee," he said, sidetracking the question. "I'm no longer the old playboy, careless Cal."

At Dee's raised eyebrow and look of skepticism, he went on. "We all have the power to change. Don't you believe that?"

"Why, yes, of course." Clearly, Annie realized, Dee had her own agenda where the company was concerned. But for now, she was still eyeing Annie. "And what about Cal's recent publicity—your ideas, Ms. Valenti?"

"Of course not," Annie lied. "All Cal."

"Matter of fact, I don't recall seeing your picture in the papers at all." Dee fixed her blue-eyed gaze on Annie.

"She's a very modest gal," Cal said, giving Annie a squeeze. "She prefers to stay out of the limelight."

"Hmm. Does she get out for family gatherings, Cal?"

"Why don't you ask her, Dee?"

That seemed to throw her off, and it gave Annie a chance to regain her composure.

"Well, Ms. Valenti," Dee said finally, "you *must* meet the family. I can't imagine why Cal hasn't taken you out to the Main Line before now."

"He's been very busy," Annie said coolly.

A waiter passed, and Dee swiped a glass of champagne off the tray. "So it seems," she said.

Cal jumped back into the conversation. "I'm busy changing. The power of change is an amazing thing, isn't it, Dee?"

Before Dee could answer, Cal turned to Annie. "You believe in my ability to change, don't you, honey?"

"Of course, dearest." Annie tried to look loving.

He grinned and gave her a kiss on the cheek. "That's Annie. Always on my side."

Dee's smile was synthetically sympathetic. "That's so important in a relationship. Trust. Support." She put her hand on Cal's arm and leaned forward, speaking softly. "I can imagine how much you needed her support after that foundling-hospital incident."

Annie could feel herself tense, but Cal stayed calm and cool. "It was hardly an incident. I just made a donation to the hospital . . ."

"And that donation got into the papers." She smiled knowingly. "As everything about you seems to do recently. Why, it's almost as if you had a photographer following around after you, Cal. It's just—magical."

"Just lucky," Cal corrected.

"In the case of the foundling hospital, I'd say it was bad luck." Dee flashed a toothy smile. "Considering the fallout . . . that nasty little article in the *Downtowner*."

Annie couldn't stay quiet. Dee *had* to bring up the one slip, the only slip she'd made. "That columnist is nothing but a gossipmonger."

Dee's attention switched back to Annie. "How sweet. How terribly loyal. But tell me truthfully, my dear, weren't you the tiniest bit upset about those dreary old paternity charges being dredged up again? I'm assuming, of course, that you knew about Cal's troubles in that regard."

Annie spoke through clenched teeth. "Yes, I knew, and I'm not at all upset," she said stoically. But, in fact, she had made a terrible mistake, pairing Cal with the foundling hospital. He'd told her to stay away from children, but this had seemed like such an easy photo opportunity that she'd grabbed at it: Cal and the administrator, outside the foundling hospital, beaming over a check. There wasn't a baby in sight, and Cal didn't even have to go into the hospital for the usual tour. But a wily reporter made the connection anyway.

Annie closed her eyes in painful remembrance. She'd never forget the column's headline and lead sentences:

Cal Markam Donates
To Foundling Hospital

Is playboy turned benefactor atoning for past indiscretions? Not long ago, Markam was vigorously fighting paternity suits, not embracing the cause of children.

"Are you all right, Ms. Valenti? You look pale."

Annie opened her eyes and looked straight into the older woman's bright blue orbs. "I'm fine. Just... thinking."

"My Annie, always using her head," Cal said, proudly.

Over his shoulder she caught a glimpse of a man with a camera. Annie beckoned to him. "Look, there's a photographer," she said innocently. "Oh, I have such a good idea. Let's get a picture of you and your aunt together. Wouldn't that be fun?"

Cal grinned mischievously. "Great fun. Come on, Dee, smile for the camera." He took her arm firmly.

"No, no," Dee protested. "My hair... really..."

"You look perfectly wonderful," Annie insisted. "Over here," she directed the photographer. "Two generations of Markams united. One happy family."

"WHAT A COUP!" Annie chortled. "You and Dee Frame together! Do you know what that means, Cal? Do you?" Annie was almost bouncing on the seat of the limousine as it cut through the cold autumn night.

Cal sat back, laughing. "No, what does it mean, Annie?"

"It means you have your aunt's stamp of approval."

"Well, let's not get carried away."

"Okay," she agreed. "It'll *look* as though she approves, and that's what counts. Oh, I love it! What an evening!"

Cal agreed. "The ballet was bearable—"

"And the girls were beautiful," Annie added. "And the fund-raiser—"

"More helpful to our cause than I'd imagined," Cal admitted.

"I love what you said to your aunt about the power to change." Annie continued to ride high.

"That was pretty damn good, huh? Course, I didn't mean a word of it."

Annie came back to earth quickly. "But you seemed sincere."

"Just as you said, it's the way it *looks* that counts."

Annie tried to hide her disappointment.

"Don't pout, Annie. I told you early on that I'd play the game as long as it took to get what I wanted. As for becoming an upstanding pillar of the very boring Main Line society, think again, Ms. Valentine."

"But—"

"Remember, Annie, I don't have to change; I only have to *appear* to change." He stretched out his long legs. "You're doing a great job making that happen."

She waved away the compliment. "Everything went well, I'll admit, but I'm not sure it was a good idea for you to introduce me as your girlfriend. That could cause complications."

"I couldn't have told her you were my assistant. Why would I bring my assistant to a ballet benefit?"

"But—"

"No way, Annie. Dee would have seen right through it. She's pretty sharp, as you noticed. That's why you came up with the assumed name, right?"

"I was just imagining her going home to riffle through the phone book and city directory, looking for a connection...."

"And that's why the simplest story is the best. One she believes: that you're my significant other. Isn't that what it's called these days?" he teased.

Annie ignored the flirtation in his voice as she settled back against the soft leather seats, finally relaxing. "If she believed it. After all, I'm not exactly your type—"

"You're a beautiful woman," he interrupted firmly. "I'm sure that's enough to convince Dee. She can easily see why I'd want to spend an evening with you."

She frowned. That wasn't the point.

"You worry too much, Annie. We're almost home-free. The next Board meeting is only a couple of weeks away. We're on a roll."

"But nothing comes easily," she said, "as we've learned. I'm sorry your aunt brought up that foundling-hospital incident. It's been on my mind for a while now. I wish I could have told her that I was responsible for getting you into that mess."

"Forget it," Cal ordered. "I have."

Annie sighed. "But I can't. I keep playing it over and over in my mind. It could have been different if I'd just chosen another event."

Cal took Annie's hand, looking seriously into her eyes. "Annie, I'm the one who was involved in the paternity suits. They were bogus, but I left myself open to them. You can't be blamed for choosing the wrong charity."

"But I knew about the stories, I should have had more sense."

"Let it go, Annie. Stewing over the past accomplishes nothing. We can't change it. All we can do is move on."

"I know I spend too much time worrying."

"You sure do. So someone wrote a nasty article about me. It won't be the first time—or the last. It goes with the territory."

"I could have lost my job over it. Bert wasn't happy, and your father was furious."

"Hell, Dad's always furious over something. No problem."

Annie extracted her hand from Cal's, but she didn't move away, and now she leaned forward toward him. "You went to bat for me with Bert. If you hadn't, I'd be history at the firm. I'm very grateful, Cal."

"Okay, so I called Bert and we talked. You're doing a good job, Annie. Now and then we clash and sparks fly, but that's what makes our partnership work." He smoothed her hair away from her face. "That's what makes *us* work. And sometimes one of us screws up.

That's life. You need to look at the big picture and not sweat the small stuff."

The limo stopped in front of the Markam town house. "I have some letters I'd like you to look at," Cal told her. "They're requests for donations and appearances. Can you come in for a while?"

"It's awfully late—"

"Ten o'clock? Are you kidding?"

"I have to be at work bright and early tomorrow, Cal," she reminded him.

"That's right. And I'm the idle rich."

"I didn't say that—"

"It's all right, Annie."

"You could send the correspondence to my office."

"Sure, I *could*. But do me a favor. Come on in. We'll have a brandy and discuss our options. Unless of course you don't want to be alone with me."

"Don't be ridiculous—"

"You *do* want to be alone with me?"

"No, I— That is, yes, I—"

"I like a woman who knows her mind," Cal joked.

Annie laughed and relaxed. "Okay. Let's see those letters."

LIGHTS GLOWED SOFTLY in the hallway of the Markam town house. Annie remembered the last time she'd stepped into this hall, frantic, anxiously waiting for a recalcitrant Cal. It had seemed cold and unwelcoming to her then. Tonight it was warm and elegant. She'd been ushered to the parlor then; tonight Cal led her to his father's study.

"I'm using it for an office." He turned on a lamp and the room welcomed her. "I'll see if Mrs. Batelle can rustle us up a drink—"

"Coffee would be fine," Annie told him.

"Won't it keep you awake?"

Annie laughed. "Only long enough to go over the letters."

"Coffee coming up." Cal disappeared through the door, telling her to relax and make herself at home.

Easy for him to say, Annie thought. His idea of home was light-years away from hers. She crossed the long room on Oriental rugs to a sofa and matching chairs grouped around a huge fireplace. Recessed in a bay window was an antique desk, complete with computer and message center.

Annie shook her head in wonder. The surroundings reeked of old money and class. Far from anything she'd ever known. She remembered the secondhand desk she'd studied on for years. She'd been so excited when her dad brought it home, and he'd been so proud of the pleasure it gave her. Could the Markams understand those feelings? She sat down on the sofa. Annie and Cal, she thought, what a pair!

He came through the door with two glasses and a bottle of brandy. "Looks like Mrs. Batelle has gone to bed. The coffeepot was empty and I don't know where she keeps the filters. Tomorrow's her day off, and she leaves early. It didn't seem fair to wake her up—"

"Good Lord, of course not," Annie agreed.

"So—" He held up the brandy bottle with a wide smile. "Whatta you say?"

"After we go over the correspondence," she suggested.

"You've got it," he said, putting down the bottle and glasses and picking up a file from the desk.

He sat down beside her, and Annie was relieved to find that the letters were just as he'd described them. Together, for the next few minutes, they sifted through requests, discussing them, putting them in order of importance, Cal as serious and interested as Annie.

When they'd finished, Annie took the file from him. "I'll check your schedule tomorrow and see which of these we can fit in."

"You're a gem, Annie. Now, what about the brandy?"

"Well—"

"It's up to you," he added.

"Of course, I'd love a brandy." Annie realized she was making too much of his simple offer. Deep down, she'd been suspecting him of having set up the evening. First, he'd seduced her into his home, then Mrs. Batelle had been conveniently fast asleep, and finally, after an intoxicating brandy, she'd expected him to make a move on her. But they'd both worked hard and now it was time to relax with an innocent drink. There was nothing more to it.

Annie sank back into the sofa, felt the warmth of the fire and tasted the warmth of the brandy. It was as smooth as silk. She took another sip.

Cal slipped off his jacket and loosened his tie. He lounged on the sofa beside her. "I like that dress." He touched the shoulder strap almost tentatively.

She didn't move away. "Thanks, but it seemed plain tonight compared to what other women were wearing."

Cal shook his head. "Not plain at all. Just short, black, and formfitting. You and your dress stood out tonight, Annie. Have I ever told you what great legs you have?"

Annie smiled indulgently. "Yes, you have." She made an attempt to pull down her short skirt and failed miserably under Cal's watchful eye.

She boldly returned his stare. She'd seen him loosen his tie and now she could see the smooth muscles of his neck. His hair was slightly tousled and his eyes...blue, intense, mesmerizing.

Their gazes had barely met when, in one smooth motion, Cal pulled her to him. With her cheek against his chest, she could hear the slow, steady rhythm of his heart and smell the tangy scent of his cologne. Was it the heat from his body or the fire that made her feel flushed and feverish?

His voice was low and calm. "You remember, don't you, Annie? Mango Inn? The hammock, and what it was like when we held each other, when we kissed?"

His body was hard and powerful against hers, exactly as it had been that night. "I—I—"

"Don't tell me that Ms. Always-In-Control Valentine is at a loss for words." His head was bent over hers. She could feel the warmth of his breath against her cheek.

"Yes, I remember," she admitted. "And this is why I haven't been alone with you again, Cal." She willed her

voice to be firm, but it was soft and breathy and not at
all steady. She remembered Mango Key only too well.
The heady kisses. The feeling of abandon. The danger
of forgetting everything and being swept away.

"Let go, Annie. Let it happen."

She looked up at him and opened her mouth to answer, but his lips were there, stemming her reply. And
she forgot what she meant to say.

Cal felt her lips, smooth as silk and sweet as liquid
honey. He touched his tongue to hers, then explored the
sweet recesses of her mouth. The sensation was wonderful. He could feel the blood rushing to his head and
his heart beating like a hammer. Her skin was hot, her
hands, arms, back, steamy to his touch. His own skin
felt as though it were burning, and his clothes seemed
restrictive.

She felt so good in his arms, small and compact,
warm and soft. He had no idea how the evening would
end, but he wasn't ready to say good-night yet. Not
now when the excitement was building inside of him,
and Annie's lips tasted of brandy and her hair smelled
like flowers.

She moved away slightly, and he looked down at her
to see eyes that were dazed, a mouth that was soft and
vulnerable. His heart gave a little lurch, one he couldn't
explain. In many ways, she seemed very young and innocent despite her tough talk and know-it-all attitude.

"We're good together, Annie. So good . . ." He let his
lips drift along her cheek to her neck and felt Annie
shiver against him.

Her voice was muffled against his shirt. "But we work together, and no matter how attracted we are to each other—"

He drew back in surprise. "You're admitting you're attracted to me? Hallelujah," he teased. Then added more seriously, "Hell, Annie, we don't have that much time left together. We should savor it."

He saw a flicker in her eyes. "This isn't right, Cal."

"Right? My God, nothing has ever been more right."

"But—"

"You agree, don't you?" He kissed her, at first softly and then more fiercely, and he felt her react. "You *know* it's right because it feels so good," he coaxed.

It did feel good, easy, natural. "Still, I should go now, Cal. It's late. We've finished our work. And I've kept the limo waiting too long."

"Don't worry. I sent it back to the garage."

Annie quickly pulled back and moved away from him, fire in her eyes. "You sent him away? Then you must have been sure I was going to stay here. That's arrogant, Cal. In fact you're the most arrogant—"

He reached out and stopped her, hands on her shoulders. "No, I wasn't sure you were going to stay. Hell, with you I'm only sure of one thing. I want you terribly, Annie. And I know you'd want me if only you weren't too stubborn to admit it."

"You sent the limo away, Cal. What if I hadn't succumbed to your charms? How did you expect me to get home?"

"I expected to call a cab for you—if that's what you wanted. And I will call a cab, Annie. *If* that's what you want."

He could see that she didn't know what she wanted. That was the problem. Her eyes were still blazing hotly; there was fire and passion—and need—in every line of her taut body.

"And tomorrow's Ms. Batelle's day off!" she continued. "I can't believe you thought I'd fall for this."

He wanted to shake her and force her to face the truth. Instead he said, "You can't run, Annie. There's no hammock to turn me out of, no ocean for a cold swim. There's just me . . . and you. I'm tired of waiting, and I know you are, too."

He lowered his mouth to hers and kissed her again, cupping her head in his hands, holding her lips to his, kissing her until he had no breath left.

Annie looked up at him through a haze of sensations. His eyes were dark with passion, and his low, husky voice sent shivers along her spine. "I want you, Annie. I want to take you to my bed and make love to you. Don't run away from this, Annie, please."

Annie knew she should leave, walk out, find a taxi for herself. She was furious at him, wasn't she? Instead, she raised her lips to his. His kisses were like a drug, addicting, intoxicating, making her forget who she was, where she was. Annie felt her body go weak. She clung to him, returning his kiss, tasting his lips, his tongue, her fingers digging into the soft fabric of his shirt.

She was crazy for getting involved with Cal. But her body was betraying her. Her pulses throbbed wildly, and a sensuous warmth began to blossom inside of her. All her being seemed to flow toward him. Their breaths were one; their bodies were joined. Cal's mouth possessed her; his arms enclosed her. She tried to speak, to regain control, but the words caught in her throat.

Cal scooped her into his arms and started up the dark staircase toward the light at the top of the stairs.

6

ANNIE CLUNG TO CAL, who carried her up the steps two
at a time. Her heart hammered fiercely as she rode a
dizzying wave of anticipation.

He kicked open the half-closed door to his room.
Light from the hallway shimmered across the bed,
bringing back vivid memories of the last time they were
in the room together, the morning when she followed
him up those same stairs, watched as he pulled off his
shirt and turned away as he unzipped his pants.

Now she knew that she wouldn't turn away.

She slid from his arms, but remained close, caught
up in a primitive need that she was powerless to control. As Cal tugged at the straps of her dress, impatient, hurried, Annie struggled with the buttons of his
shirt. Their breaths came in short gasps; their eager
fingers trembled. A wild frenzy, bordering on desper-
ation, encompassed them.

Their clothes were tangled around their feet. Cal
kicked them away, stepped out of his shoes and pulled
her to him. They stood swaying, bodies enmeshed,
flesh against heated flesh. Cal's mouth found hers, and
he lowered her to the bed. His body covered hers, but
she didn't feel the weight as he pushed her gently into
the soft sheets.

What she felt was his lips against her breasts, planting small delicate kisses, and then his tongue caressing her nipple. Annie groaned beneath him as his mouth enveloped the taut swollen tip of her breast.

The sounds that came from her lips seemed to excite him. "I know, Annie, I know," he whispered. "We give each other such pleasure...."

He let his mouth glide lower, kissing her belly button, licking the line of her hip bone, tasting the cool, smooth flesh of her thighs. Then he found the moist warmth between her legs.

What he did then amazed her totally. There was magic in his lips, his tongue, his teeth. She felt his day's growth of beard tickle her seductively, and Annie thought she must be melting, dissolving into a churning pool of pleasure.

She writhed beneath him, her hands grasping the sheets, her head thrown back, eyes closed. It was torture; it was bliss. Whatever magic he was doing to her, she wanted more and more—wanted it to last forever. She entangled her hands in his hair, urging him on.

Annie could feel the pressure building inside her, a twisting, aching need that begged for release. As she hung on the edge of ecstasy, he stopped and looked at her long and hard, then moved upward along her body until his mouth was on her breast again, hot and seeking.

She reached for him, wrapping her arms around his shoulders, and pulling him up until his lips found hers. The kiss took her into another world, where she'd never been before, a world of total intimacy as she drew his tongue into her mouth, crazy for him, crazy to be closer, closer.

She opened her eyes and gazed at Cal. He was so beautiful, his deep blue eyes, heavily lashed, looking into hers, his high cheekbones, sculptured mouth and chiseled chin. She lifted her hand and traced the line of his cheek. Her body ached for him; her skin tingled. She wanted him so.

"Touch me, Annie," he murmured. "Touch me, please."

Shyly at first and then boldly, she explored his lower body from the waist downward, caressing his hips and then reaching for the hard shaft of his manhood that throbbed beneath her touch. She held firmly and listened to his quickening breath, the gasps of excitement that thrilled her so. She loved what she was able to do to him, what she was able to make him feel. It was in his sighs, and in his words.

"That's so good, Annie, so good," he whispered. "It makes me want you all over again. You don't know how much—ever since Mango Key, I've thought about you, about making love to you. I've fantasized about what it would be like when we were finally together."

"I've thought about it, too, Cal."

"Do you want me now, Annie?"

"Yes, I do, Cal. I want you inside of me. I want you to make love to me." Annie's voice was hoarse with need, her body yearning for his. She didn't even recognize her own voice and couldn't believe she was saying the words. There was a wild, primitive desire coursing through her which she had no power to control.

He moved away for a moment. She heard a drawer open and then close. She sighed with satisfaction. There would be no awkwardness, no questions.

He returned and knelt above her, and Annie opened to him. There was a moment of unexpected sweetness and joy as Cal pressed deep inside her. They looked at each other in the half-light, eyes locking, and Cal smiled. It was such a lovely smile that Annie's heart leapt wildly, and at that moment she felt a connection so strong that it made her tremble.

Cal moved inside her, slowly at first, matching his rhythm to hers, and layer by layer Annie felt herself opening to him as his warmth spread through her and engulfed her. Annie locked her legs around him, dug her fingers into the hard muscles of his shoulders.

Their bodies were slippery and damp with passion, and as Cal's thrusts became more urgent, more powerful, Annie moved with him. Her hunger was as great as his, and she could hear the rasping of his breath and the fierce pounding of his heart.

Ripples of pleasure grew and spread through her, and Annie knew that something wonderful and special was happening. There was nothing, no one, in her world but Cal, and the throbbing waves of ecstasy that washed over her held Annie hostage before releasing her into a sweet, joyful fulfillment.

CAL FELT ANNIE shifting in the bed as she slept beside him. He opened his eyes and in the half-light could see the soft and vulnerable expression on her face. This was a different Annie, he thought, a very lovable one. He reached out and brushed her hair away from her face.

She sighed in her sleep and smiled, and that made him grin in response.

He didn't want to wake her and yet he wanted to hold her. Cal fought off the voice inside that said to let her sleep. Overcome by need, he pulled her close until her body cuddled next to his. Her eyelids fluttered; he held his breath, a little guiltily, hoping that she wouldn't wake up.

But she did, snuggling against him. "Cal . . ."

He felt the soft tickle of her hair against his chin. "Yes, Annie?"

"So good, Cal," she mumbled.

"I know. It was wonderful."

"Umm."

"You're a most surprising woman, Annie. But I've told you that before."

"Hmm?"

"Warm, passionate, and sexy. I suspected that's how you'd be, but now I know. And I like what I found out." He kissed her warm neck.

Annie snuggled closer and wrapped her arms around him. Cal liked that. It made him feel warm and comfortable.

"You surprised me, too," she admitted. "You're much more gentle . . . and loving . . . than I imagined."

Cal dropped a light kiss on her nose. "Imagined? You mean you've been fantasizing about making love to me?"

"That was just a figure of speech."

Cal hugged her tightly, and her breasts rubbed against him. He felt her nipples tighten as they pushed against his chest. "You're a shameless sensualist, Annie."

"Am I?" She looked up at him innocently.

"Yes, and something tells me you're ready to escape from your neat and tidy world." He put his mouth close to her ear. "Tell me your fantasies. I won't tell anyone else."

"I don't have any," she murmured.

"Liar," he teased. "Then let me share some of mine." He settled back against the pillows and closed his eyes. "You and I are all alone on an island, maybe in the Keys." He opened one eye and looked at her, but she didn't respond. "The sky is blue, the sun is hot. We decide to go swimming but we have no bathing suits." His hands drifted along the curve of Annie's hip and thigh. He could feel her muscles tense and then relax beneath his touch. "But we decide to go in anyway so we undress and swim naked in the waves. Warm, soft, caressing waves."

"Then what happens?" Annie asked.

"You know what. We come ashore and kiss . . . like this." His lips found hers, their tongues touched, caressed. "And then we make love. Long, passionate, sandy love."

Annie moved her arms upward around his neck. "I'm not sure about the sandy part, but—"

"Okay, I'll change the fantasy. We're in Rome—or maybe Paris. The best hotel. Champagne. Caviar. A Jacuzzi in the suite. You undress me, then I undress you. Slowly, though. First, I take off your dress and then your slip. Your panties..." His fingers slid between her legs. "Why, Annie. No panties!"

"Because it's Paris," she whispered. "I'm being daring."

"Then I kiss you . . . here and here." He touched each of her breasts with his lips. "And here." Their mouths joined in a long, unhurried kiss. Cal felt Annie's tongue in his mouth, and he sucked it greedily. Her fingers dug into his shoulders. He could hear the rapid beating of her heart, and he knew she was as excited as he.

"And then we slip into the Jacuzzi . . ."

"Warm, warm water," Annie added.

"That washes over us. So comforting. We relax in it, our naked bodies side by side. Then I turn to you and we make love, again and again. Just like we're going to do now, Annie."

Annie's hand slipped down to touch him, caress him. He felt himself grow and throb with excitement. His blood ran hot with desire, and Cal groaned with pleasure. "Oh, Annie," he whispered. "This is better than any fantasy."

She smiled up at him with a look so tender that he felt the unfamiliar lurch near his heart again.

"If it's not a fantasy," she whispered, "then it must be a dream. Yes, it has to be a dream." She turned over and pulled him on top of her. "And I never want to wake up."

IT WAS HOURS later when she *did* wake up, reluctantly, sleepily, basking in the warmth of sunlight that bathed the big bed. She reached out for Cal, but the space beside her was empty. She sat up and pulled the covers around her bare breasts, disoriented and a little confused.

Cal appeared in the doorway, hair damp from the shower, wearing jeans, a navy pullover and boots. She closed her eyes and opened them again. She wasn't dreaming now. This was real.

"So, you're awake." He walked into the room, sat down on the side of the bed and kissed her cheek.

Annie leaned back against the pillows. "What time is it?"

"After nine."

She blinked. "I never sleep this late."

"Don't worry. Today's Sunday, and you deserve a day off. We're taking it easy, and that's an order. I found the filters, so there's coffee brewing in the kitchen, and I'm going out for the papers. *New York Times, Philadelphia Bulletin*. I'll even look for your hometown paper. What is it—the *Milltown Weekly?*"

Annie teased him back. "More like the *Milltown Monthly*. Get the *Washington Post* instead. Maybe there's a government commission that needs your expertise."

Cal rumpled her hair playfully. "No *Post*, Annie. I told you, we're not working today." He kissed her again. "I put out a bathrobe for you. It won't fit, but it'll be more comfortable for a day of lounging than that little black number you wore last night."

Annie caught a glimpse of her dress tangled up with her undies on the floor. Her cheeks grew hot as she remembered their frantic rush to Cal's bed.

He kissed her again and stood up. "I'll get some pastries, too. What would you like?"

"Surprise me," she said.

"Don't I always?" he bragged.

Annie made a face but admitted, "So far."

He left her with one last parting kiss, and she stayed in bed, watching as he walked away, luxuriating in the sight of his hard, tight rear end disappearing through the doorway.

Annie stretched lazily and got up, padding to the bathroom. She turned on the light and took a good hard look at her face, her tousled hair and bruised lips.

"Oh, boy," she said to her image in the mirror. "You've really done it this time, Valentine."

But the reflection stared back at her with a wicked half smile.

Annie turned on the water, let it run hot and then stepped into the shower, thinking all the time about Cal and their night together. Never had she known such a lover, who combined tenderness and strength, passion and playfulness.

She thought of her college sweetheart. They had lived together for a while. She'd thought she loved him. There had been an innocence to their lovemaking, at times a sweet awkwardness. Making love to Cal was different. So different. She felt free and uninhibited. And incredibly sexy. Cal gave her that freedom by what he said . . . and what he did.

As Annie toweled off, she continued her dialogue with her mirror image. "It's true. I don't know where the relationship is going. And I know I was foolish to get involved. But I did it. So there." She stared defiantly at her own face. "And I'm not sorry!" Her words bounced off the mirrored walls of the huge bathroom.

Thoughtfully, she sank down on the wide ledge of the marble tub. An affair with Cal would turn out only one way, of course. She knew that. Soon, their campaign would end. And if everything went as planned, Cal would become CEO of Markam Investments and she'd move on to her next assignment. They'd drift apart, and before long he'd find another woman.

But it didn't *have* to be that way, did it?

She stood up and slipped on Cal's robe, wrapped it twice around her, vowing not to think about the future. What was done, was done. She certainly couldn't control Cal or her feelings about him. Standing there in the middle of the elegant bathroom with its maroon-and-white marble tiles, gold fixtures and subdued lighting, she thought of Cal's words on the plane. He'd told her on the flight back from the Keys to quit worrying about the destination and just enjoy the ride. Well, maybe she was ready to do just that.

Annie adjusted the robe and went back into the bedroom. Her feet were cold so she rummaged through a drawer and found a pair of white running socks. As she pulled them on, she couldn't help giggling at the picture she made—certainly not as glamorous as the women Cal usually hung out with. She pulled the socks on and padded across the room, not feeling a bit worried about how she compared to those other women. She and Cal were a great couple, and she was having a great time.

Halfway down the stairs, Annie heard the doorbell ring. For a moment, she was surprised, and then she remembered that Cal had gone out quickly and probably without his keys.

"Forgot you key, eh?" she called out. "It's lucky for you that I'm out of the shower."

She skipped down the stairs and across the foyer, excited about seeing him again even though they'd only been apart for a few minutes. Annie flung open the door.

A woman stood before her. Tall, dark-haired, the woman was wearing a broad-brimmed hat and sunglasses. She was wrapped in a heavy winter coat with the collar pulled up around her face.

Annie stood there with her mouth open, ready to say something but unable to form the words. Finding a woman at Cal's door surprised her, but what the woman held in her arms transfixed her.

The woman held two squirming, whimpering babies.

Annie stepped back, trying to hide her shock, but before she could utter a question, the woman spoke, hurriedly, almost frantically.

"Thank God I've found someone at home! I know I should have called from the airport, but I didn't want to take the time. Besides, you never know who might be lurking at airports. The paparazzi are everywhere. Is Cal here?"

"Yes, I mean no—not yet, anyway," Annie stuttered. "I mean, he's gone out to get something."

The woman just stood there, staring, not responding. She looked vaguely familiar, but Annie felt certain that she'd never met her.

"Can I come in?" the woman asked. "The babies are getting pretty heavy."

"Yes, yes, please," Annie replied, ushering the threesome into the hall, still gazing at them. This was one of the weirdest situations she'd ever been in. Annie had no cool way to react, especially when the babies—one in a pink snowsuit, the other in blue—were hoisted toward her.

"Please, can you hold them?"

Astonished, Annie obediently took one under each arm like a couple of sacks of flour.

The woman shrugged out of her coat, her hat, her glasses, and then—to Annie's amazement—her hair! She tossed the dark brown wig on top of her coat. "Whew! That was torture. Thanks," she said as she took back the baby in pink. "Now, if you could just keep holding Eric for another moment—"

Annie finally made the connection. "You're Charlotte Baird. The model, Charley!" Despite the woman's tired eyes, there was no mistaking her cloud of blond hair or statuesque figure enveloped in a clinging red wool dress.

"Yes, I'm Charley," the woman announced as she tried to fluff out her hair with one hand and shift the baby with the other.

"But why are you—"

"Why am I here? Because I desperately need to talk to Cal. He's the only one who can help me now. I have no where else to go, really."

Annie felt her stomach lurch as she tried to digest those words. But civility kept her from reacting. Instead, she led Charley into Cal's office—not knowing where else to put her.

Charley deposited her bundle on the sofa and motioned for Annie to do the same. "If you'll just slip him out of his suit," Charley directed.

Annie sat down with the baby on her lap and struggled with the zipper of the fleecy little snowsuit.

"It's easier if you lie him down," Charley offered.

Annie did as she was told. She could see only the baby's round little face peering at her from the depth of the fleece. She had an impression of big blue eyes, a rosebud mouth, dimpled chin and pink cheeks. Looking more closely she realized that the baby's eyes were deep, deep blue, and a terrible suspicion began to creep over her.

"How old are the twins?" she asked shakily.

"Four months. They were born in Switzerland," Charley added.

Annie felt compelled to ask the next question. "And the father?" she croaked in a voice that barely escaped her dry throat.

For a moment, Charley went on with what she was doing, and bravely Annie did the same, unzipping the snowsuit and managing to extract the baby from it. She lifted him out and felt with relief that his bottom was dry. With everything else that was going on, she wasn't in the mood for changing diapers.

"Oh, yes, the father. Well, that's the problem, isn't it? And that's why I need to talk to Cal."

"You mean Cal doesn't know?" Annie felt like someone had hit her hard in the abdomen, knocking the wind out of her, making it impossible to breath.

"Nope," Charley responded. "No one outside my little village in Switzerland knows. That's why I wore that awful disguise on the flight. Oh," she added, "except my nanny, of course. She dropped us off here and took the rental car to go shopping. You know, diapers, formula, all that."

Annie sat dumbfounded, holding the squirming baby, staring at Charley in disbelief.

"You're doing great," Charley told her. "Is Eric wet?"

"No, I don't think so."

"Well, Erica is, of course. Where can I change her?"

"There's a bathroom right down the hall," Annie said.

"Okay, if you'll watch Eric . . ."

"Sure," Annie answered weakly, juggling the baby in her arms.

As soon as Charley disappeared out the door Annie felt herself sink, not really sink—she couldn't do that with a lap full of baby—but certainly her heart sank when she thought about Charley and the two babies. Twins with Cal's blue eyes. And Charley was looking for him.

Could they be his babies? Of course they could, she told herself. Why else would Charley have flown from Switzerland to Philadelphia, appearing unannounced at the town house? Why else would she say that Cal was the only one who could help her? She needed the babies' father. She needed Cal!

Annie felt sick at heart. If there wasn't a very real baby snuggling in her arms, she would think this was a dream. But it was no dream; it was a living nightmare. Annie's whole world was collapsing around her. The press would find out. Hell, *everyone* would find out. It wasn't possible to hide two babies. And disguise or not, no one could hide Charley for very long.

Obviously, Cal would have to marry her. But even then the gossip would ruin everything. He'd never be CEO of Markam—

The baby began to whimper. Annie stood up and started pacing, trying to calm little Eric, cooing soft noises that she hoped were baby-comforting. All the while, inside, she felt as though she were dying. All her thoughts about the gossip, Cal's future with Markam, her own job security, meant nothing. What mattered was that she'd lose Cal. To Charley and their babies.

ANNIE HEARD Cal's key in the door and then his voice calling out. "I got two cheese danish and two—" He stopped dead still at the office door. "Am I seeing things? What the hell are you doing with that baby?"

Eric, who'd been uneasy since Charley left the room, took one look at Cal and let out a startled yell. Annie shouted over the noise. "I'm holding him, that's what." She was suddenly very angry.

"Whose baby is it, anyway?"

"Charlotte Baird's," Annie shot back.

"Charley! She's here?" Cal's expression was a mix of pleasure and surprise.

"Yes, she's here." Annie took advantage of a momentary lull in the baby's screams to lower her voice into a tight stern response. "She's in the bathroom changing your other baby. She has twins."

"Wait. Hold it a minute. What do you mean *my* other baby?"

Annie started to pace again, up and down, jiggling and patting Eric, trying to soothe him and at the same time contain her growing anger toward Cal. "She says you didn't know, but surely you suspected."

"Annie—"

She gave him no room to get a word in. "But whether you knew or not, we still have the babies to deal with. Two babies. *Two*," she repeated, as if that made him twice as guilty.

Cal dropped the pastries and newspapers on the floor with a thud. Eric, who had stopped crying, quivered in Annie's arms and let out another shriek.

"Be careful," Annie ordered. "The babies have been on a plane all night, and they're a little cranky."

"I'm starting to get a little cranky myself. What the hell do you mean by suggesting that this baby—"

"*These* babies," Annie corrected.

"—that they're mine. Did Charley tell you that?"

"Not exactly." Annie comforted the baby, holding its damp face against her cheek until the cries subsided. "Not in so many words, but why else is she here? When I asked her about the father, she said she had to see you."

"This is unbelievable. A misunderstanding..." Cal massaged his temples with his fingertips as if to clear his head. Then he fixed a hard blue-eyed gaze on Annie and raised his voice, demanding, "How could you jump to such a conclusion?"

Eric let out a cry and Annie ignored Cal's question while she jiggled the baby up and down. "You realize that this ruins the campaign. There's no way I can explain away two babies—"

"You don't have to, dammit."

"Your aunt will have a field day, and the press ..." Annie groaned. She hated to think of the publicity. "You'll have to marry her, of course." As she spoke the words, she felt a sharp pain in her heart. She wanted to yell at him, but she kept her voice calm. "The wedding, the babies, maybe all that will create a picture—"

"Are you crazy?" Cal was shouting again over Eric's cries. "I'm not marrying anyone."

"That sounds like the Cal Markam I know—and love," Charley drawled as she walked into the room carrying the other baby. "Hello, darling."

7

CAL RUSHED FORWARD to hug Charley and then stopped, moving first to the right and then to the left to avoid the bundle in her arms.

"Dammit, Charley, I can't get close to you."

Charley shifted the baby to one side and extended her cheek.

Cal managed a kiss. "What the hell is going on?" he asked.

"Motherhood, darling, and it's grand and glorious." She thrust the baby toward Cal. "Here, hold Erica while I rescue my son. He doesn't seem happy at all." Charley reached out and relieved Annie of her bundle.

A surprised Cal dangled Erica in his arms. She looked up at him coquettishly, her deep blue eyes curious. Then a smile appeared on her tiny rosebud mouth. Cal reacted predictably, smiling back.

"Is that a smile I see on the man who dislikes kids so much?" Annie asked.

"Well, I—" Cal gazed down at the cooing baby.

"Well, you—" Annie prompted.

"This is some cute baby," Cal replied.

"And she obviously knows her father," Annie snapped.

"Her *what*?" Charley seemed nonplussed as she gazed at Annie over her son's head.

"Father," Annie repeated adamantly.

"Oh, no, you don't think—" Charley began.

"That he's their father? Of course, I do. You don't have to hide it. That's why you're here, isn't it?"

Charley looked from Annie's stricken face to Cal's confused one and smiled slyly. "Tell her, Cal, darling."

Annie didn't wait for Cal's explanation. She turned on her heel and started toward the door. She didn't have the slightest idea where she was going—without her clothes, a coat or her purse. But she was going.

"Annie!" Cal's stern voice stopped her in her tracks. "Listen to me. I'm getting angry now."

"*You're* getting angry!" Annie couldn't believe her ears. "A beautiful, world-famous model has just arrived with your two babies at the very time when we were about to complete your image change and—"

"They're not my babies. Tell her, Charley."

"Well . . ." Charley smiled as coquettishly as her daughter.

"Dammit, Charley, this isn't funny," Cal said. "Quit playing games. These are not my babies, and you know it."

Charley looked at him with wide-eyed innocence. "I never said they were."

"How old are they?" Cal demanded.

"Four months."

Cal smiled broadly. "And their names?"

"Eric and Erica." Charley was laughing back now.

"I'll be damned. Named for Rick."

"In a way," Charley admitted.

"Ol' Rick is a daddy. Well, what do you think of that?"

From the doorway, Annie looked from one to the other with confusion.

"Who else but Rick?" Charley replied philosophically. "But it was fun to tease you and your . . . friend."

"Uh, my friend," Cal repeated. "I guess you two haven't met officially. Charley, this is Annie Valentine. She's my very suspicious public relations consultant."

"That's supposed to be a secret, Cal," Annie said as she wrapped the oversize robe more tightly around her and tried to act as if she always conducted business in a silk bathrobe and white tennis socks.

"I doubt if Charley will call any Markam Board members."

"I'm good at keeping secrets," Charley said with a nod toward the twins. "But public relations, Cal? Could it be that you're looking for a new image, darling?"

"Maybe. Something like that," Cal replied easily. "Having to do with the family business. Boring stuff."

Annie, wrung out from tension and now weak with relief, didn't bother to argue. Cal's make-over couldn't compare to the glamorous Charlotte Baird and her two adorable babies.

"I want to hear all about it," Charley said.

"Not a chance—at least not until I hear about you and the babies." Cal was awkwardly holding Erica, who seemed quite content as she gazed at him with adoration in her round blue eyes. "Let's sit down."

"There are two bottles of juice in my diaper bag in the hall. If someone would—"

Annie realized that she was the only adult in the room without a baby in her arms so she went to fetch the bottles. Eric's had a blue nipple, Erica's a pink one. Annie brought them back, handing the pink one to Cal. He was stiff and obviously uncomfortable but managed to hold Erica upright enough that she could take her bottle. Eric settled contentedly in his mother's arms.

"So, talk," Cal ordered Charley.

"It's a long story, but I'll start at the beginning. You knew that Rick and I were having a tough time back in California last year. I wanted to get married and he wasn't ready. We had mammoth fights on the subject. To allow some cooling off time, I went to Europe for a photo shoot. That's when I found out I was pregnant. I decided to stay there."

"And you didn't tell Rick?" Cal asked.

"Of course not. I didn't want him to be forced into marrying me. I certainly wasn't hard up for money." She tossed her head and gave Cal her million-dollar smile. "Thanks to you."

Cal shrugged, and Charley directed the next remarks to Annie. "He gave me my start. If it hadn't been for Cal, I'd still be bopping around the beaches. Because of him, I'm financially independent. I knew I could easily support a child—or children, as it turned out."

"Money or not, you still want to marry Rick—"

"Sure."

"And if I know Rick, he would have married you in a minute if—"

Charley shot a bemused look toward Annie who smiled in return. "Men," she said. "They just don't get it. So let me explain, Cal. I want Rick to marry me, yes, but because he *wants* to, not because he *has* to. Get it?"

"I'm not a total idiot, Charley. Sure I get it."

Charley winked at Annie. "So I did everything on my own. I rented a house in a Swiss village near Bern. I found a nanny for the babies." She paused. "I guess that's British—nanny, but I don't know the Swiss word. Anyway, Fräulein Greta is great. Sixty-four but very spry." Charley laughed musically, shaking her mane of hair again.

"All right, Charley," Cal said. "You can call me sexist or macho or whatever you want to, but I still say that you love Rick and he loves you. What about that?"

Annie didn't want to get involved, but she realized that Cal was right. "It must have been difficult," she said finally, "not to tell Rick that he was the father."

"It was," Charley agreed. "It still is. About two months ago I heard through friends that he still missed me and wanted to see me. So I wrote him. Then he called me. We talked for hours, and to make a long story short, we're meeting in New York tomorrow."

"Good for you," Cal said.

"If we still love each other, if we can work it out—"

"Are you going to tell him about the babies?" Annie asked.

Charley moved her lovely shoulders in an eloquent shrug. "Hmm, not exactly. I want to see him alone first. If that goes well, then of course I'll tell him."

Annie felt a sudden sense of dread. She'd been sympathetic to Charley, understanding, but now she began to think ahead and see something that could be very threatening. She put her dread into words.

"I expect you'll take the babies to New York with you?"

Charley's eyes were round with innocence. "How can I possibly do that?"

"Well—" Annie was nonplussed.

"Why, the press would have a field day. Remember, I had to use that hideous disguise to get out of Europe without the world knowing that Charley was on her way home. Unmarried. With two babies. So you see, I can't possibly take the babies to New York...."

Annie's worst fears were being confirmed. Knowing what was coming next, she sank onto the sofa and waited.

"So I thought—" Charley turned pleading eyes toward Cal. "I thought about you, darling. You have power and money—and a town house that's built like a fortress which your parents hardly ever use. No one would look for the babies in Philadelphia of all places. And it's only for a few days. And of course, Greta will be here to take care of everything. She's incredibly efficient."

Cal was stunned. "Don't tell me you're asking me to baby-sit for the twins."

"Of course not, darling. I know all about you and babies. No, I just want you to provide space for them. That's all. I'll feel very secure when I know my babies are in the care of their mother's—and father's—best friend."

Annie couldn't believe what she was hearing, and she couldn't keep quiet. "A hotel seems like a better idea," she suggested. "A nice one with all the amenities."

"Wait a minute," Cal cut in. "It's one thing to be hesitant about baby-sitting, but it's another to refuse a friend."

This was a complete turnaround, and Annie was shocked.

"Friends of mine don't go to hotels," Cal declared. "Not when I have an empty house."

Charley sighed. "I knew you'd come through for me. I've never been away from the twins, and to leave them in a hotel—well, it would be hideously impersonal. What kind of mother would do that?" she asked.

"Don't worry," Cal assured her. "The third floor is empty. There're two bedrooms and even a kitchen up there. It should be perfect for the kids and the nanny—"

"No!" Annie stood up abruptly. "It's out of the question for the twins to stay here." She directed her objections to Cal. "I can't believe that you'd consider such a thing. There's no way we could keep two babies a secret. The servants would find out. The family would find out. And worst of all, the press would find out."

"Annie," Cal warned.

"No, Cal, please don't interrupt me. I've been hired for a very specific purpose, which you and I both understand full well. If the babies stay here, everyone will think they're yours, and I'm not going to allow that. It's not even a possibility."

"I don't understand—" Charley began.

"Then let me explain Cal's situation to you," Annie said. "We're approaching the end of a complex PR campaign. Cal is on a wave of great publicity which hasn't even peaked yet. We can't take any chances.

These babies—" She gestured helplessly. "Just one photo, one rumor that there are babies hidden in the town house could ruin his chance to become CEO of Markam."

"I didn't realize that," Charley admitted.

"There's no way you could have," Annie said, "but now that you understand—"

Charley looked from Annie to Cal. "I understand that there could be a PR problem. But I also understand that lots of things seem to have changed. The old Cal wouldn't have cared what anyone said or thought. Friendship meant something to him. But please don't worry, Ms. Valentine. As soon as Greta comes back with the car, we'll find a hotel."

Charley's voice was filled with hurt, and Annie saw the glimmer of tears in her eyes. She felt awful about that, but there was nothing to be done. Someone had to tell Charley the truth.

Cal interrupted the women's exchange. "I'll repeat what I said. There'll be no need of a hotel." He got up, slowly and carefully so as not to disturb Erica, who was dozing against his chest. His voice was low and firm. "Annie, I'd like to talk privately with you."

Annie bristled. She felt like a misbehaving child called into the principal's office. Shoulders tight, head high, she marched down the hall to the parlor ahead of Cal. He closed the door behind them gently.

Then she turned to him. "What's the matter with you? Don't you understand what it would mean to our campaign if two babies were discovered hidden in this house? Besides," she added, "you don't have any idea how to care for babies."

"No, I don't," he admitted. "But in your hysteria you're missing the point—Rick and Charley are two of my best friends and I'd do anything to help them out."

"But not this—"

"Yes, this." He was adamant. "If Charley wants to keep the babies a secret from Rick for a few more days, then I'm damn well going to oblige her. Mrs. Batelle knows how to be discreet."

"It won't work," Annie insisted stubbornly. "It'll backfire. Can you imagine the fallout? Everyone who sees those babies will think they're yours. Everyone will—"

"Maybe *everyone* isn't as suspicious as you, Annie," Cal responded through clenched teeth. "Or as willing to jump to conclusions without knowing what the hell is going on. You were quick to assign paternity to me."

Annie wouldn't back down. "I can only judge by past history, and you're no saint, Cal."

"I never pretended to be, but I expected some loyalty from you."

"I wasn't hired for my loyalty, Cal, but for my expertise. What I have to offer is good advice. Don't get involved in hiding these babies."

Cal stood his ground. "I've told you before that I don't desert my friends, and Charley and Rick are friends. That's the bottom line." Cal leaned back against the library desk. "I appreciate your concerns, but this is private and personal. The decision is mine, not yours."

Annie's face flamed in anger. "So you're disregarding my advice and getting entangled in this ridiculous charade? Doesn't my opinion count—don't *I* count?" Her voice rose uncontrollably.

At that moment, little Erica awoke with a start, struggling against Cal's chest, her face screwed into a frown, her pink lips puckered.

Cal began to pace, patting the baby's back, obviously unsure what to do next. Erica squirmed in his arms, looked directly at Annie and started to whimper. Startled, Cal followed the baby's gaze to Annie. "Don't you see? We're talking about two little babies—"

"And your old friend, Rick, and your old life—which has nothing to do with me," she blurted out without thinking. "After last night, I hoped I might be part of your life. What a fool!"

"Annie..." His voice softened. "This isn't about you and me—"

"Oh, yes, it is." The words were wrenched from her. "And I get the message. Stay out of your personal life, take care of business, act like the paid employee I am. Fine. I'll be happy to stay out of your personal life—and out of your bed."

"You're overreacting," Cal said. Erica had settled down and was snuggling against his shirtfront.

"No, I'm not," Annie argued back. "I'm thinking very clearly, which is more than I can say for you." With that, Annie turned on her heel and crossed the room, opening the parlor door. "I'm going upstairs to get dressed now, and then I'll leave you—and your babies."

Before he could answer, she went out and slammed the door behind her.

Annie could hear Erica's piercing cry halfway up the stairs. Good, she thought. Let him charm the baby out of that.

MONDAY MORNING DAWNED gray and cold, and Annie's mood matched the weather. Her anger at Cal had turned into something much more debilitating, a combination of anxiety and dread. And she had good reason for worry.

They were in the homestretch with just over two weeks to go before the board meeting, and in that time anything could happen. Especially with two babies ensconced in the town house. Anyone could discover Cal nursemaiding Charley's babies. Anyone could jump to the wrong conclusion—as she had.

The story could blow sky-high. Annie was good, but she doubted if she was good enough to put a positive spin on this story.

After finally realizing that the babies weren't Cal's, she'd felt relief. But not for long. Cal wasn't the father, but Cal was willing to do anything for the mother, and he certainly had no intention of listening to Annie. She was sick at heart over their argument, and dreaded facing him.

But after an almost sleepless night, she had come to terms with her anger, which she knew was really hurt. Annie realized that she'd opened herself to Cal, become vulnerable. For so many years, she'd reined in her feelings, struggled to prove herself, do what was right. That was the only way she knew to be successful and get out of the dead end that was Milltown. She didn't have family background or business connections. But she had drive and a will to succeed, and hard work never daunted her. Then Cal came along and told her to loosen up. Let go, have fun and enjoy the ride.

Annie's mouth curved in a bitter smile. She'd followed his advice, and look what had happened. Charley arrived with the babies, and he turned away from her toward his friend—with no thought of what that would do to his relationship with Annie.

He'd ignored Annie's advice, and that made her feel unimportant and left out. The truth was, she was more the saddened lover than the irritated businesswoman.

In fact, Annie was behaving childishly. Foolishly. Like a woman in love. That was tougher than anything else to deal with. As she was falling in love with Cal, everything was falling apart.

She moved like a zombie through her workday, accomplishing very little. She asked her secretary to call Cal and remind him of the breakfast speech on Tuesday. She didn't want to talk to him yet because she was afraid of what she'd tell him. The truth. That she was falling in love—and she was jealous of Charley and the babies.

But why? Because the babies had somehow taken a place in his heart—in the heart of this man who didn't even like kids.

To the amazement of the office staff, Annie left work early. Too tired to shop for groceries, she picked up a pizza for dinner and curled up on the sofa in her apartment, staring at a flickering TV screen and seeing nothing.

THE FRANTIC PROGRAM chairman for the Greater Philadelphia Young Executive Club met her the next morning at the door of the hotel meeting room. Cal was
scheduled to speak in less than five minutes, and he
hadn't shown up!

Did Annie know where her boss was?

"Delayed by the weather," was her quick, smooth
comeback. "The streets were so icy, I left my car at
home and took a taxi. He'll be here," she promised,
smiling with much more self-assurance than she felt.

As soon as the anxious woman turned back to the
meeting room, Annie made a beeline for the pay phone.
What the hell was he up to now? she wondered. Was he
trying to punish her for her angry words, or had he
simply forgotten?

That last possibility didn't seem at all likely. She held
her breath and punched in Cal's number. She'd know
the answer soon enough.

Mrs. Batelle answered the phone after half a dozen
rings.

She sounded harried and out of breath. In the background, Annie could hear the babies crying. Loudly.
Furiously.

That wasn't a good sign.

"Where's Cal?" Annie shouted into the phone.

"At the hospital."

"The hospital?" Annie sagged against the wall.
"What happened? Is it one of the babies?" Or Cal? she
thought suddenly.

"It's Fräulein Greta," Mrs. Batelle said. "She fell
down the third-floor stairs early this morning. Cal rode
in the ambulance with her. Her leg is broken, there's no

doubt about that, and it looks bad to me. The bone was—"

"Mrs. Batelle," Annie interrupted, "what about the babies?"

"Well, you hear them, don't you? I can only feed one at a time without help. I was going to call out to the Main Line house and ask them to send someone into town, but Cal said I couldn't tell anybody about the babies. I don't know what that's all about, except it makes my job much harder."

"I'll be right over." Annie made the statement automatically. "As soon as I talk to Cal. We'll hire a nanny— or something."

"Well, I certainly hope so. I'm too old to be a mother again." The background crying intensified. "I better hang up now and see what I can do. Please, don't forget I'm here alone with these babies!"

After volunteering so readily, Annie had no idea what to do next. Should she tell the program chairman that Cal wasn't going to show due to an emergency? And what about the TV crew? They were pushing through the lobby with cameras and expressions of urgency. They didn't usually cover the Young Executive breakfast meetings, but today Cal would be here, and that was news.

Annie decided to call the hospital.

"Damn," she said aloud. She'd forgotten to ask which one. Annie dug in her purse for another quarter to call the town house. It was 9:05. Across the lobby, the program chairman stood outside the meeting room. Annie waved cheerily and tried to look as if nothing was wrong. Club members were filing in, finding their seats. Waitresses were pouring coffee.

And Mrs. Batelle wasn't answering the phone. Finally, the machine picked up. Frustrated, Annie slammed down the receiver and started across the lobby.

Just then Cal surged through the revolving door in a puff of cold air, taking off his overcoat and gloves as he sprinted toward her.

"Greta broke her—"

"I know all about it," Annie said. "I talked to Mrs. Batelle."

"Who is probably hysterical about now," Cal added as they walked toward the meeting room. The program chairman lit up when she saw Cal, and the cameras began to whir.

"Hysterical is the exact word," Annie agreed.

"Could you—" Cal looked at Annie pleadingly.

"I'm on my way to the town house now."

"Thanks," he said as he reached out to shake proffered hands, adding over his shoulder, "I'll see you back there in about an hour."

"STOP! Don't ring the bell," Mrs. Batelle warned as she pulled open the front door. "I heard your taxi drive up." She let Annie inside. "The boy just went to sleep but this one—"

Erica gurgled against Mrs. Batelle's shoulder, her hands balled into tight little fists as she sucked on her pacifier.

"You're awfully good to take all this on." Annie pulled off her coat.

"I didn't have much of a choice, did I?" She made an attempt to take Annie's coat.

"That's all right. You have your hands full," Annie told her.

"That I do. I can't be expected to work two jobs, and Lucy's on vacation until next weekend. Cal says he'll try to hire a new nanny today. That can't be soon enough for me."

"What about Charley—"

"Who's he?"

"Charley's a female, and she's the twins' mother."

"He didn't mention any mother to me." She thrust Erica into Annie's arms, trading her for the coat. "The phone's ringing. I don't want the other one to wake up," she explained, rushing toward the library.

Annie was left standing in the hall with a less-than-secure hold on the baby. Little Erica squirmed. Annie struggled to hold on. "I'm not real good at this, Erica, so please cooperate, and I won't drop you. I hope."

Erica looked up with what appeared to be suspicion. Her pacifier fell to the floor and the corners of her tiny mouth turned down. Annie knew something was coming, and it wasn't going to be good.

She tried to ward it off. "It's me," she cooed. "Remember . . . on Sunday." No, that wasn't a good idea. Erica hadn't liked her on Sunday, either. Annie chuckled to herself. As if the baby understood! But it was the tone of voice that mattered, not the words, she told herself. "I'm really a very nice person, Erica. I was just a little cranky then. You know the feeling."

Erica creased her pink forehead into a frown, and Annie jiggled her gently. "You'll have to take my word for it."

Mrs. Batelle appeared at one end of the hall, her face flushed. "That was Mrs. Markam. She and Mrs. Frame are on their way over."

"Here? Why?" Annie stopped jiggling Erica.

"One of those charity luncheons."

"But here? Without giving you any notice?"

"They were supposed to meet at Mrs. Frame's, but a kitchen pipe burst, and so the caterers are on the way over here—and so are the ladies. And I sent Lucy on vacation because everything was so quiet at the town house!"

Annie had only one concern: she couldn't let the ladies—especially Cal's Aunt Dee—see the babies. She had to take Mrs. Batelle into her confidence.

She spoke quietly, conspiratorially. "Cal has a very good reason for not wanting anyone to know the babies are here, Mrs. Batelle. They're his friend Charley's babies, and she's in New York with their father, to patch things up—or something." Annie shrugged. "It doesn't matter. What matters is that the ladies might jump to conclusions."

Mrs. Batelle was nodding vigorously.

"Maybe I could explain this to Cal's mother, but his aunt—she'll go into orbit."

"Mrs. Frame does tend to look on the dark side," the housekeeper confirmed.

Annie was oblivious to the whimpering Erica in her arms or the worried face of Mrs. Batelle. All she could think about was Dee, whose eyes had gleamed with malicious pleasure at the ballet party when she brought up the scurrilous paternity suits. Annie knew Dee wouldn't hesitate to start rumors—even plant a story—about the babies. Especially if she found out that they were Charley's. The nightmare that had begun on Sunday with Charley's arrival was intensifying.

"How much time do we have?" Annie asked. "Maybe I can get the babies to a hotel or something—"

"Fräulein Greta's rental car is in the garage," Mrs. Batelle said.

"Great! We can load everything into it and go—well, somewhere. Get out of here, anyway." She handed Erica back to Mrs. Batelle. "Can you give her a bottle or something so she won't cry? I'll start packing up their things."

"There's a ton of stuff," the housekeeper said. "Portable cribs, formula, diapers, toys, clothes."

"Don't worry, I'll find it all," Annie said, taking the stairs two at a time.

THE DOWNSTAIRS HALL was filled with baby paraphernalia. Eric, dressed for the cold weather in his fleecy snowsuit, was wide-awake. Annie had deposited him on his back, and like a fat little insect, he kicked his arms and legs, trying desperately to turn over, a trick he'd yet to manage.

As for Erica, she was drowsy, almost asleep, and as hard to dress as a rag doll, Annie thought as she struggled to get the baby into her snowsuit. "Do they ever sleep at the same time?"

"I've never seen it," Mrs. Batelle answered. "But let's not worry about that now. There's no time. Mrs. Markam has to drive in from the Main Line, but Mrs. Frame lives right here in town."

"We're almost ready. I found the car keys. I'll bring it around and we can load up and then—" Annie had no idea what she would do after that.

The sound of a key in the lock caused both women to jump guiltily. But it was only Cal. He strode in and stopped short when he saw the jumble in the hall. "What the—"

"Your aunt's on the way," Annie told him quickly, "and your mom, and who knows how many Philadelphia socialites."

Cal raised his eyes heavenward. "Not the Federated Women's Charities?"

"The same," Annie told him.

"Then we are in trouble. I remember Dad talking about this. Their current project is raising money for the hungry at Thanksgiving."

"Your father? Is he coming, too?"

"Probably," Cal said. "Mom insists that he get the ball rolling every year with the first donation." He picked up a portable crib and an overstuffed diaper bag. "Keys to Greta's car?"

Annie handed them over.

"I'll bring it around so we can load up."

IN LESS THAN FIFTEEN minutes the car was loaded. Annie had strapped Eric into his car seat and returned to the hallway for Erica. Cal was waiting at the curb in front of the town house, motor running. It was like a getaway from the scene of a crime, Annie thought. She wanted to laugh, but she was afraid to give in to the desire. If she started laughing, hysteria might take over, and she wouldn't be able to stop. Later, she promised herself. There'd be time to laugh later.

"Be careful going down those steps," Mrs. Batelle warned. "We don't want another broken leg."

"Don't even think about it," Annie said as she inched down the steps, clutching the rail, Erica in one arm, a diaper bag over her shoulder. "Thanks for everything." Suddenly, Erica woke up with a vengeance, screaming mightily. Annie searched for the pacifier.

"Oh, no!" She remembered it dropping from Erica's mouth. "The pacifier—it's in the hall. If Dee sees that—" Annie rushed back up the stairs and headed into the hall.

Mrs. Batelle was there before her, triumphantly holding the pacifier. "I'll just rinse it off quickly." She was gone less than thirty seconds, returning with the pacifier, which Annie grabbed as she headed for the door again. "Good luck with the lunch—"

When she reached the top step, her mouth dropped open. For some inexplicable reason, Cal was driving away!

Annie waved frantically with her free arm and opened her mouth to shout his name when she recognized the woman coming down the street toward her. It was Dee Frame, striding along in an ankle-length cashmere coat and fur hat.

Annie ducked back inside, looked around, wondering where to hide.

Mrs. Batelle was there instantly. "What—"

"It's Dee. She's coming up the stairs. Cal made a clean getaway. But I—"

"Give me the baby," Mrs. Batelle said.

"Okay." Annie passed the baby to the housekeeper. Then she reconsidered. "No! What if she sees you with Erica? She'll know something's up!" She reached for the baby.

Mrs. Batelle held on firmly. "But what if she sees *you* with Erica? She'll *really* think something's up. At least this can't be my baby!"

"That's true." Annie released her hold on Erica. "But if you're holding Erica, Dee's sure to think it's Cal's baby and he hid her with you. I better take her." Annie reached out again.

Mrs. Batelle managed to keep her hold on Erica. "Or she'll think it's Cal's baby that he hid with you. And that you're the mother!"

"Oh, damn. Damn." Annie was trying to decide what to do when Dee flung open the door. "No one answered so I just—"

Annie had won the struggle for the baby.

"It's Miss Valenti, isn't it?" Dee's eyes flickered with curiosity.

"Mrs. Frame. How nice to see you," Annie lied.

Erica, obviously cranky from being wakened from her aborted nap and then pulled back and forth, stuck out her bottom lip and flailed her arms.

"Why, I didn't know you had a baby," Dee said.

"No, no. I don't. She's—"

Mrs. Batelle stepped forward. "My niece's."

Unfortunately, Annie came up with her own explanation at the same time. "My cousin's."

Dee's eyes were bright with curiosity. "Why, Ms. Valenti, then you and Angela are related?"

"No. Except by marriage, of course," Annie added triumphantly. Pleased that she'd come up with an explanation, she plunged ahead. "That's how I met Cal. Through my cousin."

"Who married my niece." Angela backed her up.

"How quaint and old-fashioned," Dee commented. "And where is the darling boy now? Cal, I mean."

"At a meeting, I think, but he has nothing to do with all this," Annie said.

"We were just baby-sitting and—"

"Here at the Markam town house?" Dee asked. "That's seems strange, especially considering Cal's feelings about babies."

Annie looked around. Mrs. Batelle had disappeared, and she was on her own to deal with the problem.

"It seems a little strange," Dee continued, "that you're here with the baby of your cousin—or Mrs. Batelle's niece, or whatever—"

"Don't worry about Mrs. Batelle. She just wants to help," Annie said vaguely. "Now it's time for us to go—"

"Do you live nearby?"

With her blue eyes boring relentlessly into Annie's, Dee could certainly make an innocent person feel guilty. "Not really," Annie confessed. "But I love to walk." She realized that her performance was deteriorating by the minute. Who would be walking for fun on a cold, gray day, carrying a baby? "And my cousin lives nearby," she added quickly.

Dee smiled and seemed to let her off the hook. She had other things on her mind, Annie saw. She was gazing at the baby, touching her cheek. "Such lovely blue eyes."

"Just like my cousin's," Annie stated.

Dee's eyes flicked back to Annie. "Are you and Cal still an item?" she asked over the baby's head. "He seemed so fond of you at the ballet gala."

"We're good friends," Annie said with a nervous laugh. "Now, I really must take the baby back to her home."

"Your walk, yes, of course," Dee said, her smile as icy as the November air. "Even in the little snowsuit, this weather can't be good for the baby." Obviously, she was determined to keep Annie here until the whole charity group—including Cal's parents—arrived.

"I'm a mother myself," Dee said. "There's no love like the love for a child. I absolutely adored my darling Glen as a baby. And even now . . ."

Annie hiked Erica higher on her hip. How much did the child weigh, she wondered? And how in the world did Charley manage with two babies? But that wasn't important now, not when Dee Frame was adding it all up. Annie. Cal. A baby. An early-morning exit from the town house. It was obvious that Dee wasn't about to let Annie get away easily.

As Annie had hoped, Mrs. Batelle came to the rescue. "Mrs. Frame, the caterers have just driven up to the back door. I think you need to speak with them. There's been a mistake with the quiche."

Dee's lips tightened. "Not for long," she said. "I don't accept mistakes." She turned to Annie. "I'm sorry about this inconvenience. We must do lunch very soon and talk about Cal—and babies." She flashed Annie one of her deadly smiles and disappeared down the hall.

After letting out a deep breath, Annie opened the door, holding Erica firmly in her arms. Then, standing on the top step, she looked down the street and with relief saw Cal waiting at the corner.

She walked to the car, calmly, in case Dee was watching from the window. When Cal opened the door, she quickly strapped Erica into her car seat, then collapsed beside Cal. "Let's get out of here."

"Sorry about driving away," he apologized, "but if Dee had seen you and me and two babies fleeing from the town house, she would have had a field day."

"I don't think she believed a word I said."

"There's more bad news," Cal told her. "My parents passed me in their car on the way to the garage. I'm not sure if they saw Eric or not—"

"Great, just great." Annie shook her head dejectedly. "The trouble with babies is that you can't hide them."

"And speaking of that," Cal said, coming to a stop at a red light, "where are we taking the babies?"

Annie sighed. "My apartment—but just for a few hours. We're going to call their mother and tell her to get back to Philadelphia." She glanced at Cal. "That is what we're going to do, isn't it?"

8

CAL PAUSED in the kitchen door of Annie's apartment, the portable phone in his hand. An unexpected picture met his eyes. The living room was bathed in light, illuminating the highly polished, wide-planked floor and adding warmth to the bright, slip-covered furniture. Annie was curled up on her overstuffed sofa, holding a baby. There was no way Cal could have known which baby except for the blue sleeper. It was Eric, and he was cooing. Annie seemed to be caught up in the moment.

It was quite a picture, Cal thought as he watched Annie cuddle the baby, echoing his coos. The sunlight poured across them. It painted them with a golden glow and added a softness that almost took Cal's breath away. The woman and baby were a beautiful picture. Clearly, Annie was taken with little Eric and the baby with her. Holding him, she looked a million light-years away from the businesslike, hard-driving woman she made herself out to be.

She glanced up at Cal and then quickly back at the baby. "Eric's not sleepy at all. In fact, he wants to stand up. Look at this, Cal."

Holding the baby firmly under his arms, she planted his little feet on her thighs, and he squealed with delight. "If I let him settle down a little bit, he can almost stand. Watch this." She let the baby's weight settle onto her thighs but still held tightly on to him. He wobbled but squealed with glee. "I wonder if this is harmful? His legs seem kind of bowed out." She was talking to Cal but not taking her eyes off the baby.

"Aren't babies bowlegged anyway?" Cal asked.

"I guess so," Annie answered as Eric bounced and laughed.

"If it hurt him, he'd cry. He seems happy enough to me," Cal observed as he dropped into a side chair and stretched out his legs. He couldn't remember when he'd been as tired as he was now. "Babies are a hell of a lot of work," he said.

"Well, they'll only be here for a short while," Annie said. "We'll have plenty of time to recover."

When Cal didn't respond, she asked, "You did make the phone calls?"

"Yes."

"And everything's arranged?"

"Not exactly," he equivocated.

Annie settled Eric onto her lap. "Charley's not coming back to get the babies?"

"I can't really answer that because I haven't been able to find Charley. She left a message saying she and Rick were close to working things out and wanted to be alone."

"Alone where?"

"That's the problem. Apparently they were going to a cottage somewhere in upstate New York. Unfortunately, she didn't say where."

"Surely she'll call to check in," Annie offered.

"She will, but unfortunately she'll call the town house."

"And if Dee answers—"

"I told Mrs. Batelle to try to beat Dee to the phone, but if my aunt's the slightest bit suspicious—"

"And what happened today certainly has aroused her interest. But what about Fräulein Greta? Does she have any instructions for us about the babies?"

"I didn't talk to her," Cal replied.

Annie shifted Eric in her lap. "Why not? I thought you were going to—"

"Hold on a minute, Annie, and let me explain. Greta's under sedation. According to the doctor, she'll be able to talk to us tomorrow."

"What do we do in the meantime? We need to know about these babies now—what they eat, what they drink. Between the two of us, we don't know anything. It's the blind leading the blind, Cal."

"They drink formula," Cal said confidently. "We know that because there're about fifty cans in the kitchen. They won't starve."

Annie was still dubious. "What about real food—like cereal or fruit? Vegetables?" she said. "You always see babies at this age eating food from those little jars—"

"There are none of those little jars, as you call them, with their stuff. Obviously, they've survived on formula."

"A qualified nanny will know for sure. You did find someone, didn't you?"

"Not exactly—"

"Cal, that was the most important call, to the agency for a new nanny. For today. Don't tell me we aren't getting one. This is an emergency."

"They don't have emergency nannies."

"Surely, someone—"

"None of the agencies provides that service. But two of them promised to send some candidates over tomorrow morning for us to interview."

"Tomorrow morning! Didn't you tell them how desperate we are? How unprepared we are? Didn't you—"

"I did my best to sound desperate, but tomorrow is the best any agency can do."

Annie panicked. "What's going to happen in the meantime? Neither of us knows the first thing about taking care of babies!"

"I understand it's instinctive . . ."

"For mothers, maybe. Neither of us is a mother, Cal. We're surrogates, and there's nothing instinctive about us."

"Then we'll do the best we can," Cal offered.

"Here, at my apartment?"

"Unless you want to pack them up and move all their gear somewhere else."

Annie settled the baby against her shoulder. "Nope. I don't want to go through that again. So we'll stay here and do the best we can. But only for tonight. After that, you find a nanny and the four of you can go back to the town house until Charley reappears. If she— Good Lord!"

"What's the matter, Annie?"

"You don't suppose she's dumped these babies on you for good, do you?"

Cal laughed loudly, startling Eric, who looked for an instant like he was going to start screaming. But Annie managed to quiet him with his rattle. "There, grab this, and try to ignore the man's crazy laughter," she said. Eric caught the rattle and banged it against Annie's chest.

"Ouch!" She shifted him higher and turned back to Cal. "You don't even like kids—"

"Not kids in general, but these two are different. More interesting than most—and very intelligent."

Annie tried to hide her grin. "Well, I'm glad you think so because you're about to be saddled with them."

"Annie, don't be ridiculous. Charley'll be back. You have to stop looking on the dark side."

"Fine. As long as you promise not to leave me alone with these babies." She looked up at him pleadingly. "You won't leave me alone, will you?"

Cal didn't answer for a moment while he let that request sink in. He saw a look on Annie's face he'd never seen before. He'd seen her soft and vulnerable side with the babies. But this was different. "Are you saying you need me, Annie?"

"Of course. I need you to help take care of these babies. One person can't possibly handle them alone. I need—"

"Me? You need me," Cal said softly. "And I'm certainly not going to leave. You and the babies and I can be quite happy here. It's very pleasant. I like this apartment."

"Do you really like it?"

"I sure do," he told her. "I like old buildings like this with big airy rooms. Was this an old town house?"

"Yes," Annie told him. "It was renovated and then made into three apartments, one on each floor. I like the floor-to-ceiling windows. In old buildings there's always lots of natural wood and rough brick. I took advantage of that."

"You did a great job." There wasn't a lot of furniture, Cal noticed, but what there was had good lines. It was straightforward and honest. Just like Annie.

"It's not very big," she said dismissively. "Not like the Markam town house."

"All that brocade and mahogany can become boring," Cal replied. "I've told you I'm not a snob, Annie. I like this place. Nice living room and bedroom and a really spacious kitchen—which reminds me, I'm starving." He looked at his watch. "Three o'clock. It seems like midnight, and I haven't eaten since last night."

"No breakfast?"

Cal shook his head. "A quick cup of coffee."

"Me, too," Annie said. "And the bad news is there's nothing to eat in that spacious kitchen. Except baby formula."

Cal groaned. "I'll pass on that. One of us has to make a food run. And since you're playing mommy to Eric, I guess that someone's me." He got to his feet and stretched his tired muscles. "Nearest market?"

"Balducci's—two blocks east."

"Any special orders?"

Annie thought for a moment and then shook her head with a grin. "Nope, just food and lots of it. And Cal, you will come back, won't you?"

Cal laughed as he leaned over to pat her arm. "Don't worry, Annie. I'm not going to desert you."

"ISN'T THIS STRANGE, Erica?" Annie whispered. "You and Eric and Cal and me together in my apartment, playing house." She kept her voice low so as not to disturb Eric, who'd fallen asleep just before Erica woke up. "So far, I've been lucky with only one awake at a time, but I'm still waiting for both of you to sleep at once."

Annie struggled diligently with Erica's wet diaper, pulled it off and then went about the changing ritual. She was getting pretty good at it, she thought as she secured the tabs and gave Erica's bottom a pat. "There!" She tossed the wet diaper in one pail and the sleeper in another.

"Laundry could be a problem soon, but I expect the new nanny will handle that. I'm going to leave it to her."

Erica's lip trembled as Annie pulled on the sleeper. "You'll love the new nanny. We'll interview them all very carefully and find the perfect choice. She'll be a combination of Mary Poppins and Nana. You remember Nana, don't you? The dog in *Peter Pan?*"

Erica regarded Annie with her solemn blue eyes. "Guess not," Annie said. "Well, come on." She snapped the legs of the sleeper and picked the baby up. Carrying Erica into the living room, Annie looked down at the little girl. "Will you ever smile at me, Erica? You smile at Uncle Cal all the time, but—"

At the first chime of the doorbell, Annie was there, flying across the room while still holding tightly to the baby, hoping that the other one didn't wake up.

"Eric's asleep—" she began.

"What's happening, Ms. Valentine?"

"Oh, Ted," she said, greeting the grocery delivery boy.

"Yep, it's me. Got your groceries, but, whoa, didn't know you had a baby."

"I'm just borrowing her, Ted. Put the groceries in the kitchen while I look for my handbag." Annie began to scurry around.

"Chill out, Ms. Valentine. The guy who bought the groceries tipped me plenty." Ted plopped the box of groceries onto the kitchen counter. "He said to tell you that he had a few errands to do, but he'd be back as soon as he could."

For a brief instant Annie panicked; then she remembered his promise not to desert her. "I'm sure he just needs to stretch his legs a little and get some fresh air," Annie said, half to herself.

She thanked Ted, waved him out the door, and began to unpack the groceries, a task she found difficult with only one free hand. Erica was snuggled in the crook of her arm, cooing happily.

"Just stay content, Erica. I know you don't love me a lot, but let me get the groceries unloaded, at least."

Erica was noncommittal so Anna hurried to unpack what looked like the makings of an Italian feast—fresh pasta, sausage, tomatoes, shredded Parmesan and two kinds of lettuce for salad.

There was also a bakery box, which Annie peeked into. Cannoli. She could feel her digestive juices churning. Like Cal, she'd had nothing since the early-morning coffee. She wondered if he could cook. Cal in the kitchen. Like Cal with babies, it didn't compute.

As she was putting the vegetables away, she heard him call softly from the hall, and when she got to the door he was whispering hopefully, "Are they asleep?"

"One up, one down." Annie opened the door, and Erica bubbled with delight at seeing Cal.

"Hi, girls. Miss me?" He dropped one of his bags on the sofa. "Books on the care and feeding of babies. They should have all the answers we need."

Annie opened the bag and thumbed through the top book. "Or at least get us through the day until we hire a nanny. This one's illustrated. That's helpful. Kind of like those how-to books on home decorating and—"

"Cooking. Which I'm going to do right now." He pulled a bottle of wine from the other bag. "And to make the occasion festive, here's the best bottle of Italian red I could find." He held out his arms. "Come here, Baby Erica. You can help cook."

Eagerly, the baby went to him with a big smile, and Annie couldn't believe what she was feeling. Jealousy. She tried to ignore it. "*You're* going to cook?"

"I have many talents, Annie. I thought you knew that. Not only am I going to cook, but the result will be the meal of your life."

"I can't wait," she said a little dubiously.

"And over dinner, we're going to talk," he announced firmly.

"We need to," she replied. "I missed a whole day at the office, and we have the rest of your schedule to plan—"

"Not about work or my schedule. We're going to talk about us, about what's going on."

ANNIE WAS A LITTLE uneasy about Cal's suggestion. But she soon realized there was going to be no time to talk during dinner. There was hardly time to eat.

Eric woke up just as Erica dozed off. Cal settled the sleeping baby into her Portacrib while Annie warmed a bottle for the hungry one. Then, just as they sat down at the table and Cal took his first tentative bite, Erica decided she was hungry, too.

Annie couldn't believe it when she heard the cries from the pink-ribboned Portacrib. "She hasn't even been asleep an hour."

"She didn't have her afternoon bottle," Cal reminded Annie. "I'll warm it up this time." He handed Eric over. "If you get him in the right position, you can lean over him to eat."

But Annie couldn't make it work. "There's only one solution," she said when Cal returned with Erica and her bottle.

"I know. Eat in shifts. I'll feed both babies while you gobble down dinner."

"And I'll burp them while you eat."

"Agreed," Cal said.

"And if you put them to bed, I'll wash dishes."

"Putting to bed means changing diapers, right?"

"Yep," she affirmed.

"Something tells me I got the wrong end of this bargain—no pun intended."

DARKNESS HAD FALLEN by the time both babies were asleep, but now that there was an opportunity to talk, Annie decided she could claim exhaustion. In fact, she wouldn't have to just claim it; she *was* exhausted.

And because she was so tired and confused, she'd probably end up making a fool of herself and let it slip how she really felt about Cal. And she didn't want to do that as long as she had no idea what his feelings were. Did he think of her as a business associate, someone to help with the babies, or as a woman he was attracted to? Right now, she really didn't *want* to know.

So when Cal came out of the bedroom and into the kitchen, she made it clear that she was ready to get some sleep.

"Okay," he said, "but how do we work out this sleeping thing?"

"The babies in their Portacribs. Me in my bed and you—"

He saw her glance into the living room. "On the sofa?"

"On the sofa," she repeated. "It's comfortable, and if I need you during the night—"

"If you need me, I'll be ready," he said with a wide grin.

"I mean if I need you to help with the babies. I can't believe that both of them are actually asleep now—at the same time. Maybe they'll sleep all night."

"Yeah, and maybe Aunt Dee will be canonized as a saint. So, do you want to be first in the bathroom?"

"I think so—before I fall asleep on my feet. I'll shower and be right out."

Annie rushed through her shower and put on her heaviest flannel gown, covering it with a flannel robe. Nothing seductive, nothing suggestive.

Being careful not to wake the twins, she crept into the living room.

Cal looked up from a book at her, an amused glint in his eyes. "Is that what the successful young businesswoman wears to bed? Her grandma's nightie?"

Annie bristled, not at his teasing words but because she was sure he knew what she was up to in hiding behind the flannel. "I find the material very comforting," she told him.

"And the long socks?"

"Sometimes I have cold feet."

Cal grinned. "Yeah, I know."

"Sorry I can't come up with flannel pajamas that would fit you."

"Nothing left by ex-boyfriends?"

Annie shook her head. "Sorry."

"That's quite all right, Annie. I don't sleep in pajamas. Never have."

"Well, then . . ."

"I sleep in the buff. Remember?" He looked up at her with a sexy glint in his eyes which Annie tried to ignore.

"I see you've been reading the baby books," she commented.

He handed her one of them. "Please note in chapter two, 'Although many pediatricians put babies on strained food very early, milk is all they really need for the first four to six months.' So you can quit worrying about that." Cal headed for the bathroom.

"Don't wake them," Annie cautioned.

Cal laughed. "Believe me, I'll avoid that at any cost."

Ten minutes later, when he reappeared, Annie was deep into the baby book. She glanced briefly at Cal, looked back at the book and then quickly at him again, her jaw dropping. He wore nothing but a towel, wrapped low around his hips. She found herself taking in his strong legs, muscled arms, and broad chest with its sprinkling of golden hair. Then she looked away quickly.

He sat beside her on the sofa and picked up another book, which he began to flip through. Annie got a whiff of the warm soapy scent of him. His hair was still damp from the shower, and his skin gleamed golden.

She got up quickly. "I'll bring you a pillow and some blankets. You can read in bed, but you'll probably drift off quickly if you're as tired as I am."

"I'm beat," Cal agreed. "Taking care of babies is harder than running a business." He stretched his arms high and then linked his fingers behind his neck. The gesture caused every muscle in his arms and chest to ripple and bulge. Annie hurried for the linen closet.

As she rummaged around for an extra pillow and sheets, her flannel robe and nightie seemed very warm. She couldn't get the image of Cal out of her mind. Even though she was more tired than she'd ever been in her life, even though she was involved in a crisis that could end her career, she couldn't think of anything except Cal Markam's body and what it had felt like next to hers.

"Stop it," she warned herself. "You need to get some sleep, not to think about Cal. Pretend he's not here. Pretend—"

She entered the living room and tossed the bed linens to Cal. Then she turned and fled to her room.

THREE HOURS LATER, Annie and Cal were shouting at each other, not in anger, but over the wails of the babies. Both Eric and Erica were awake, and from the sound of their cries, extremely unhappy. Even Erica, who usually responded to Cal's soft words, was screaming until she was red in the face.

"I don't know what to do," Annie said, as she marched up and down trying to hold on to Eric's squirming body. "Maybe they're sick."

"Both of them at the same time? Seems unlikely." Cal, wearing only his underpants, was trying just as desperately to hold on to Erica, who bowed her body as she screamed.

"Let's check out the books again, maybe there's something we missed."

"I told you what the books say," Annie shouted back. "Check their diapers. We did. Check for pins. We did. Check for scratchy tabs in their clothes. We did. We also fed them and changed them and sang to them and walked them—" Her voice trembled. "I don't know what to try next, Cal."

"Maybe they have croup?"

"What is croup, anyway? I never figured that out," Annie said.

"Look it up."

"If you hold Eric." Annie handed him over, and Cal became totally buried in screaming babies.

She thumbed through the books and came up with an answer. "An inflammation of the respiratory tract accompanied by hoarse coughs and labored breathing. Hmm. I don't see any evidence of that."

"Could they be teething?"

"At four months? Isn't that a little early?"

"Don't ask me, Annie. Look it up."

Annie flipped through the books again. "I'm afraid they're too young. First teeth usually begin to erupt at about six months."

"Well, they could be *anticipating* the problem." Cal fell onto the sofa, struggling to hold on to both babies. "I just don't get this. They seemed so . . . so contented when they went to sleep. Maybe it's delayed jet lag. Maybe in Switzerland, they'd just be waking up."

"So what do we do, give them coffee and donuts for breakfast?"

Cal tried to rearrange the babies. "Your attitude is less than helpful, Annie."

"Sorry. None of this was my idea, but I've done the best I could, Cal. Now I'm at my wit's end. The neighbors will probably start beating on the walls soon."

Cal struggled with the babies, especially Erica, who seemed incensed over having to share him with her brother. Her ferocious crying got Eric off on a tangent of his own.

"All right," Annie said, totally frustrated. "I'm going to look up sleep problems in all the indexes, then, in an organized fashion—"

"You're nothing if not organized, Annie," Cal said over the noise.

She gave him a withering look and turned to her books, reading each entry. "Okay, this one says we should let them cry it out, put them in their room and shut the door, and eventually—"

"Eventually all of Philadelphia will be banging on the door. Besides which, the babies will be traumatized. I don't like that idea at all."

Annie tossed the book aside. "Me neither. It seems cruel to desert them like that. How would you like to be left all alone in your bed—"

Annie could hear his laughter over the crying, and she realized the naiveté of her question. "Never mind, I know your answer." She riffled through the pages of another book. "This doctor has a totally different suggestion. He says that babies need the bodily warmth and comfort of their parents. Babies cry because they feel lonely and insecure—"

"Are you suggesting you and I and the twins all pile into bed together?" Cal was pacing up and down, a crying baby under each arm.

"I'm not suggesting it, the doctor is. Maybe if we were all together, relaxed, peaceful . . . Oh, I don't know. Maybe Erica and Eric are picking up our stress, and until we relax, they can't." Annie felt on the verge of tears herself, as if everything were closing in on her and she had no control.

"I'll try anything," Cal said. "Lead the way."

He followed Annie into the bedroom where she peeled back the covers on her bed. "How do we do this?"

"Hmm. Let's see," Cal said tiredly. "I guess boys on one side, girls on the other. Hell, I don't know. I'll lie down on this side, and you lie down over there. We'll put the babies between us and see what happens."

"Well, put Erica next to you—she's bound to be happier that way."

"Okay, so it's boy, girl, boy, girl."

Moments later, Annie lifted her head from the pillow, listening to the ceaseless crying. "It's not working," she declared.

"Give it time," Cal said. "I think Erica is slowing down a little. Notice how she hesitates longer between screeches?"

Putting her head back against the pillow, Annie listened. "I think you're right. Eric has sort of lapsed into a hiccuping stage, haven't you, baby?" Annie moved closer so that Eric lay in the curve of her body. "Cuddle up closer," she ordered Cal. "She needs to know you're there."

Cal pulled Erica close to his chest.

"Maybe babies are like cats," Annie said sleepily. "You know how a cat will lie on your chest to hear the beat of your heart and feel your breathing? Maybe babies are like that."

"Like a cat . . . Okay, nice kitty," Cal said, stroking Erica's face. "You've always been on my side. Do your best now and stop crying."

Erica gave one last tremulous sob and lapsed into silence, cuddled tightly against Cal's chest.

Eric continued to sob, but softer. "I think he'll drop off soon. I really do," Annie said hopefully.

"I'm not moving," Cal said. "I don't want to do anything to upset the balance."

Annie touched Eric's forehead. "His skin is so soft, like a petal. They really are sweet babies, aren't they?"

"When they're asleep," Cal said.

"I think they like to hear us talk. As long as we don't argue."

"Who's arguing?" Cal asked. "I'm too tired to argue."

"Me too." Annie looked across the pillow at Cal. His eyes were closed, and one of his big hands rested on Erica's diapered bottom.

Annie felt a soft warmth flow over her. She was seeing Cal Markam as she never had seen him before, probably as no one had ever seen him. Suddenly she felt a great wave of tenderness for him, a feeling so strong that she had to reach out to him.

"I'm sorry, Cal," she said in a low voice.

"Not your fault about the babies," he murmured.

"I don't mean that. I'm talking about the argument we had. I behaved childishly. I guess I was jealous of Charley and her past with you. She was so chic and beautiful and she has known you for years—"

Cal raised his head from the pillow and looked at her. "Annie, I'd just made love to you. Did you think I would dismiss you so easily?"

"Yes! That's the problem. I thought you were choosing her and your old friends over me." Now that it was out in the open, it seemed much less important somehow.

Cal touched Annie's cheek with his free hand. His fingers were warm against her face. "It's not about choosing, and I never meant for you to feel left out. Making love to you was glorious, Annie. It was special and wonderful. Don't you ever doubt that, promise?"

"I promise." Annie brought his hand to her lips and kissed his fingers. "I felt the same way."

"When this is all over, how about the two of us going away somewhere special? No babies, no Aunt Dee, no Markam Investments. Just you and me and a great big bed."

Annie snuggled down into the mattress. The babies were both quiet now, their breathing deep and regular. Cal stretched his arm across her, enclosing all of them in a cocoon of warmth and intimacy.

She smiled and gave Cal's hand a squeeze. "It's a date, Cal. Just you and me."

9

ANNIE AWOKE BEFORE DAWN. The bedside lamp was glowing in the dimness of the room. Cal slept on his back, one bare leg sticking out from the covers. To Annie, he looked young and vulnerable and engagingly sweet.

Eric had scooted up from his position on Annie's chest and was sleeping happily draped over her outstretched arm. As for Erica, she had started out sleeping cuddled next to Cal on her tummy. She was still beside him, asleep on her back.

"Your sister turned over by herself," Annie whispered to Eric. "All by herself."

Eric slept on, but Erica opened her eyes at the sound of Annie's voice. She studied Annie in her serious, solemn way. Annie forced a nervous smile. "You turned over, little girl. Did you know that?"

Erica wrinkled her forehead, and Annie braced herself for the familiar frown followed by tears. Instead, miraculously, Erica smiled. A wonderful, sunny, warmth-radiating baby smile. Annie felt a tingle behind her lashes. Erica was smiling. At her! Chortling under her breath with joy, she looked from Eric to Cal, who were beginning to stir.

"Hey, boys," Annie said softly. "You won't believe who just smiled at me."

"So WHAT DO YOU THINK?" It was now noon, and Annie was slumped on the sofa with Erica asleep against her shoulder. She and Cal had just completed a marathon interview session with three nannies.

Cal lifted Eric to his shoulder and began to pat him gently on the back. The burping process with Eric was long and drawn out, and Cal knew he'd need all his patience.

"I'm not sure," he said tentatively. "No one comes out as a clear winner."

"Then we have to do it logically and in a business-like way," Annie decided. She shifted Erica and reached for her notepad. "Mrs. Morant was first. She was the rather large lady—"

"I remember. Do I remember! Formidable, I'd call her."

Annie consulted her notes. "But she's had a lot of experience. Nanny for over 25 years. I'm sure her references are excellent."

Cal stopped his patting for a moment. "But what about her idea of letting the babies cry it out? When we told her about putting them in bed with us, she was horrified."

A smile curved Annie's lips. "And she thinks we're married. What if she'd known the truth?"

"She would have stormed out without finishing the interview." Cal shook his head. "Awfully rigid."

"Well, we don't have to tell her everything."

"Just the same, I'd hate to think about both of us gone and the babies lying in their little cribs crying."

Those kinds of comments by Cal didn't surprise Annie anymore. He was hooked. And so was she. Annie looked down at the sleeping Erica, stroked her downy cheek with one finger and said softly, "I can't stand to think of that, either. Let's eliminate Mrs. Morant."

Cal agreed. "What about Inge?"

"Oh, yes, Inge." Annie glanced up to catch his expression, but she was too late.

With a straight face he said, "I think she has potential."

"I bet you do." Annie didn't have to look at her notes. "Blond, six feet tall with the body of a Valkyrie. Could her skirt have been any shorter? Or her boots any taller? Next to her, I feel like Cinderella."

Cal looked Annie up and down. "Quite a Cinderella."

"Sure, dressed in an old jogging suit stained with spit up on my shoulder, barely combed hair and no makeup—"

"I like the natural look."

Annie tried to keep up the humor, but she couldn't help letting a little jealousy get in the way. "She's tall and blond, a recurring theme in Cal Markam's life."

"No reason why tall women can't take care of babies."

"She's very young."

"Not much younger than you," Cal reminded her.

"But not as . . . well, stable," Annie argued.

"How do you know?"

"Look at all the jobs she's had." Annie ran down the list. "Baby-sitter in Sweden, au pair in London, nanny in New York . . ."

"Working her way around the world like lots of Europeans. There's nothing wrong with that."

"Cal . . ." Annie warned.

"Okay, she's a little flighty." He paused. "*Very* flighty."

"And not mature enough to care for our . . . I mean Charley's . . . babies."

"Okay," he agreed, "Inge is out."

That taken care of, Annie relaxed as Cal became momentarily distracted. "Good boy, Eric," he said with a grin. "Did you hear that burp, Annie? This kid is something." Cuddling Eric, he babbled a few words of baby talk, caught himself and looked up, embarrassed. "Eric really likes me to talk to him like that. It makes him smile."

Annie smiled, too, enchanted with the scene before her. "Now, back to the list—and Cissy Halpern. Right age, good references." Annie frowned. "She seems to love babies . . ."

"So, why the frown?" Cal sank back on the other end of the sofa.

"I think she likes them a little too much, don't you? All that oohing and aahing over these two."

"We oh and ah," Cal pointed out.

"But we do it within reason, and because we know how precious the twins are. She was indiscriminate. Overblown."

Cal was thoughtful. "So, you think she has some ulterior motive for being a nanny, like maybe she craves a child of her own or maybe she'll kidnap the twins? Annie, could you have been watching too many television movies?"

"Okay, maybe I'm being a little dramatic, but she was definitely overeager. Remember?"

"Yeah, the way she came on so strong to Eric without giving him time to adjust, chucking him under the chin and babbling to him. I don't think he liked her at all."

Annie agreed. "And Eric's our friendly baby." She didn't mean to say 'our' and added quickly, "I know Cissy's highly recommended, but I have bad vibes about her."

"I was doing okay until she told us she wants to change their feeding schedule. Start them on cereals and fruits right away. I told her that the books say some babies' digestive systems aren't well enough developed to have cereal until the fifth or sixth month, but—"

"I'll bet she's the kind who will stuff them with food to keep them quiet," Annie said darkly.

Cal slumped against the sofa, closed his eyes and groaned. "So, where does that leave us? I can call another agency—"

"Do you really think they'd have any better choices on such short notice? Let's face it. All the good nannies are taken."

He slowly opened his eyes and peered at her. "Do you mean what I think you mean?"

"What could that possibly be?" Annie asked innocently.

"That you don't want to hire anyone to take care of these babies. You want us to do it, don't you?"

Annie's shoulders sagged. "It wasn't my original intention, Cal, I swear. I wanted a nanny as much as you did. I'm sure you remember how I resented the twins for their interference. It bothered me that they could just show up and overturn our lives." She smiled down again at Erica, who lay sleeping beatifically in her arms. "But they also *turn over!* Like Erica did last night, remember?"

Cal nodded. "She's a genius. No doubt about it."

"And she smiled at me. After all that, after being so close to them, how can we hand them over to strangers?"

Cal sat up. "We can't, not when they've just gotten used to us—"

"Bonded with us," Annie corrected.

"Bonded," he repeated. "And to desert them… Hell, Charley'll be back soon. There's no reason we can't handle the babies for a few more days."

Annie's eyes were wide with amazement. "I can't believe we're saying this."

"I can't, either," Cal agreed.

"But we are, aren't we? We've fallen in love," she went on. Then, seeing a quizzical look on his face, added hastily, "With the babies."

His expression was unreadable. "There's no doubt we've fallen in love—" He hesitated and then, instead of qualifying his words, let them hang in the air. Their eyes held for a moment before they both looked away.

She tried not to notice the half smile that lingered on his lips.

"What about your work, the office?" Cal asked.

"My secretary can messenger over all the correspondence, and I can return phone calls from here. That is, if you can hang around to help with the babies."

"Sure. I can do that. But I need to go home first, get a change of clothes and see if Charley has called. If not,

I'll try to track her down. And I need to check on Fräulein. Can you handle the babies for an hour or so?"

"As long as one of them sleeps, but don't be gone too long. And pick up something for our lunch—"

"Yes, ma'am."

"Oh, and would you bring that list of requests for speeches from your house?"

"Yes, ma'am." Cal responded with a laugh. "Sergeant Annie, in charge again."

"An exhausted sergeant. Maybe when you get back, I can have a nap. Then you can have one. Wouldn't that be glorious?"

Cal leaned over and kissed her cheek. "A nap together with no babies in the bed would be a lot more glorious. A nap with no clothes on. In fact, before the nap we could begin to take off our clothes and—"

"Cal, please! Not in front of the babies!"

"SNEAKING OUT on us, son?"

J.C. Markam stood in the living room doorway of his Philadelphia town house, puffing on a large cigar.

Cal stopped at the bottom of the stairs to comment, "I didn't think Mom let you smoke in the house."

"She doesn't, but she's not here at the moment. Dee and your mother are at one of those charity meetings." He waved his son into the living room. "We came into town yesterday just as you drove off. Where've you been?"

Cal decided to be vague. "Working, kind of."

"Hmm." J.C. was contemplative. "I hope you're still walking the straight and narrow, Cal. Especially now that you're on a roll. The speech at the Young Executive Club went over very well. I got a few calls about it," he explained. "But we have to keep the ball rolling. I assume your Miss Valentine has more irons in the fire."

Cal smiled at the mixed metaphors. "I'm sure she does, since I've never seen a woman work as hard," he replied honestly. "She's practically exhausted from the effort, but she's still hanging in." They both were, babies and all, Cal thought.

J.C. nodded. "We made a good choice with her. Or rather I did, since as I remember, you were a little hesitant."

"Live and learn, Dad. Annie has turned out to be much more than I expected." Cal edged toward the door, ready to leave.

But his father wasn't finished. "Course, your Aunt Dee is trying to stir up trouble about her. Miss Valentine was here at the house yesterday—with a baby, she says. Very suspicious, she says."

"She says, huh?" Cal laughed. "Dee can make any situation look suspicious."

"The baby is somehow related to Angela, she says."

Cal laughed. Then the idea made him suddenly nervous as he began to wonder what the housekeeper had revealed. "I guess Dee gave Mrs. Batelle the third degree."

"Tried to, but Angela hung tough." J.C. chuckled. "She was a closemouthed clam in her answers. Talked about the sad circumstances the family was going through. Dee couldn't make head nor tail of it. Or figure out how Miss Valentine was related to Angela. What do you know about that, son?"

"Not much, I guarantee you, Dad." Hoping that would end the conversation, Cal moved toward the front door again.

"Your mother finally had to order Dee out of the kitchen so the caterers could work. But Dee's a damned bulldog after a bone when it comes to digging up the dirt on you."

Cal smiled. "Wouldn't a ferret be more appropriate?"

"You get the point, son. She's on to something, and that something is connecting the baby to you, proving Angela and Miss Valentine are lying. If I know Dee, she's hot on the trail of a paternity suit. Now, son—" he puffed on the cigar "—it just wouldn't be good for your image for a baby to pop up now."

"Don't worry, Dad. The situation is under control."

"But I do worry, son, about everything, now that the Board meeting is closing in. I don't want to be surprised by sleazy tabloid headlines ruining everything we've worked for."

Cal met his father's eyes evenly. "I haven't fathered a baby, Dad. I swear to that. Dee's just fishing. Don't let her get to you."

J.C. blew a smoke ring and watched it dissipate in the air. "Course, your mother and I have our own questions about the baby *we* saw—in your car. We didn't mention it to Dee. But it seems we're dealing with two babies, both of them belonging to Angela's niece, I suppose?" Skepticism dripped from the older man's voice. "This is exactly the wrong time for you to be caught with a baby under each arm, especially when you're so secretive about them. That in itself is suspicious as hell. Course, I'd never mention it to Dee."

For a moment Cal thought about telling his father the whole story, but he knew that would just open a dam—as the older man would have said—of questions and warnings Cal didn't have time for.

"The baby situation is a complicated one," he explained, framing his next words carefully. "One baby, two babies—it doesn't really matter. The important fact is that neither is mine despite the rumors Aunt Dee's stirring up. I want you—and Mom—to believe that." Cal put his hand on his father's arm and looked him straight in the eye. "Trust me a little longer. I won't let you down, not when we're so close to our goal."

J.C. covered his son's hand with his own and said in a voice gruff with emotion, "You've never really let me down, son, not even during your nudie-cleaning-service period. I've always known you'd do the right thing. After all, you're a Markam." Then, as if embarrassed by his demonstration of affection, he turned away and stubbed out his cigar. "So, where're you off to, dressed like that, the gym?"

Cal glanced down at his sweats and sneakers. "Sure, a little workout and then a little work—with Annie. We have some unfinished business to take care of."

J.C. turned back too late to see the mischief in his son's eyes. "Good, good. Make every moment count."

"I definitely plan to, Dad."

ON THE WAY BACK to Annie's apartment, Cal stopped off at the grocery store. He could cook only two meals— the Italian one and a stir fry he'd learned from a Eurasian woman in California, one of the few brunette Surfer Babes. As he headed for the vegetables, he thought about how much had changed since California and those days and nights with Sun-Li. Here he was—at least for the next few days—a family man, shopping before hurrying home to the children.

As he handed his purchases to the grocer, he realized the scenario wasn't one he'd ever imagined, and knew that long-term it would have a hell of a lot of drawbacks. But for a while it was a kick. The babies, although troublesome, were adorable and brought out feelings in him that were strange and new. And interesting to explore.

As Cal headed for Annie's apartment, thinking about the surprising changes in his life-style, he also thought about how Annie had surprised him again, too. She'd resisted caring for the twins with a vengeance. After twenty-four hours, she was totally under their spell. What was it she said? That she'd fallen in love with them.

Fallen in love.

Cal supposed he had, too. Fallen in love with the whole situation—Annie, the babies, playing house, keeping it all a secret. It was a wonderful, exciting game that appealed to his playful, romantic side.

But deep down, of course, he knew that it was only make-believe.

ANNIE HAD BEEN hovering by the door, listening for his footsteps, and the minute she heard them, she silently drew him in.

"Shh," she advised as Cal followed her into the kitchen. She closed the door and told him softly, "We can talk here."

"Don't tell me—"

"Yes!" she said excitedly.

"They're asleep?"

Annie nodded. "Both of them. But there's no telling how long it'll last."

"Sorry I took so long, but I made a few phone calls, and then Dad caught me leaving the house."

"Bad fallout?" Annie was opening bags and disbursing groceries. She held up a package. "Oh, curly noodles."

"For a stir fry, my *other* recipe. As for Dad, everything's cool."

"And Dee?"

"That's a different matter," he admitted. "She's asking all kinds of questions about the babies, giving Mrs. Batelle the third degree. She's probably trying to track down the mysterious niece right now."

"I'm sorry I involved Mrs. Batelle, but it seemed easier to lead Dee toward her—and away from you."

"Absolutely," he agreed.

"Maybe Dee'll lose interest." She sighed. "Fat chance, huh?"

"No chance, but you can relax because there's good news. There was a message from Charley on my machine. She and Rick are on their way back to New York City." Cal began putting vegetables in the crisper.

"Is that all she said?"

"She was pretty cryptic. Afraid of eavesdroppers, I guess. But I left your number at her hotel. She'll call when they get in."

"Oh," Annie said. She stared out the small kitchen window into the pale November sunshine. "So, it's almost over. I guess no matter what Charley and Rick decide, she'll come back for the babies."

Cal slipped his arms around her waist and gently turned her toward him. "You sound sad."

"I'm not," she denied. "The babies should be with their mother. I know that, but—"

"You'll miss them? So will I, Annie. Now that we have the hang of it, playing family is kind of fun."

"Everything seems to be ending at once—the babies, the campaign..." Her voice trailed off, leaving the next thought unspoken.

"Not everything, Annie." Cal cupped her face with his hands, ran his thumbs along her jawline and massaged her neck with strong fingers. Annie sighed deeply, and Cal moved his hands to her neck and shoulders, rubbing, kneading. "Tense."

"I know." Annie lowered her forehead against his chest.

"Relax, Annie."

She found herself doing just that as his fingers dug comfortingly into her rigid muscles.

"Better now?" Cal moved one hand down her spine, gently examining each vertebra through the fleece top of her warm-up. "This calls for a little closer contact." His warm breath fluttered against her ear.

Cal slipped his hand beneath her top, exploring carefully. Then she heard his breath catch in his throat. "No bra, Annie. Into our fantasy again?"

"Yes. No. I mean, I didn't have time," she murmured. She felt herself weaken and melt toward him. His body was warm and strong, his hands hypnotizing in their steady, rhythmic pressure.

Their bodies were molded together from thigh to shoulder as if no amount of contact was enough. Annie put her arms around him and raised her face, slowly, toward his. He was an irresistible force that was impossible for her to resist.

That's when he kissed her, languidly, thoroughly, exploring her mouth with his tongue and lips. Annie liked the way he kissed, as if he had all the time in the world, as if there weren't babies sleeping in the bedroom.

"The twins . . ." she muttered against his lips.

"They'll stay asleep long enough for me to kiss you. And maybe even longer."

He put his hands on her hips and then cupped her bottom and pulled her closer. Annie felt the hardness of his erection pressing against her. "Cal, I don't think . . . The bedroom . . ."

"Who needs a bedroom to make love?" He kissed her again, more urgently.

"No, I mean, the babies in the bedroom—"

"They're asleep, Annie. And we're awake. Very much awake. I want to make love to you. Right now. Right here. I've been thinking about it all day, ever since we woke up together in your cozy bed."

"Cozy and crowded," she mumbled against his chest.

"But we're alone now, and as I said," he slid his hand back under her top, "we don't need a bedroom—or a bed—to make love." He moved his hand across her breasts.

Annie's skin tingled, and a slow heat began to flame inside of her. "You're crazy," she whispered.

"I know," Cal replied. "And I think it's catching." He guided her hand to his erection. Annie fumbled with the string on his sweats, untying it finally, even though her hands shook and she was weak with desire. Cal kissed the line of her chin, nibbled at her neck, blew into her ear until her senses were ready to explode.

Cal leaned over, hands locked behind her thighs, and picked her up, settling her onto the table. He pushed her top above her breasts, his mouth greedily seeking one swollen nipple and then the other. Fierce excitement ignited at those sensitive spots and traveled like wildfire through her body. She lay back on the table and heard the silverware crash to the floor, a bowl of fruit tumble and fall, oranges and apples rolling crazily across the tile. She didn't care. All her energy was directed toward Cal and the wonderful things he was doing to her.

She entangled her hands in his thick crisp hair, pulling him close, kissing his lips. His body was hard on top of hers as they struggled frantically to free themselves of their confining clothes.

Annie finally heard it. The shrill ring of the kitchen phone. She raised her head.

"Ignore it," Cal ordered in a gruff-sounding voice. "They'll call back."

Annie tried to blot out the sound. Her body was trembling with need for Cal, but over the persistence of the phone she heard something else—Eric's shrill cries.

With a muffled curse, Cal rolled away and reached for the phone while Annie, struggling with her clothes, headed for the bedroom.

She scooped Eric out of his crib. "It's all right now, I'm here," she whispered, cuddling him under her chin. "We don't want to wake sister, do we?" She tiptoed toward the door, her warning falling on deaf little ears as Erica let out a happy gurgle, kicking her legs, waving her arms.

Annie retraced her steps to Erica's crib. "You're laughing at me, aren't you? Eric's wet and crying, and you think it's funny that I have two babies to take care of. Well, hold on. Your turn is next."

Annie placed Eric on the bed and changed his diaper speedily. "I'm getting pretty good at this, aren't I?" she bragged. Eric stopped crying and looked at her good-naturedly.

Then Erica began making the kind of noises that demanded attention. "Okay, okay," Annie responded. "I'll change you when I settle Eric back in his crib."

That wasn't agreeable to Eric, Annie realized when he started to yell the moment she put him down.

"Here, try this until I get your bottle ready," she said, trying to insinuate his pacifier into his resistant mouth. He was having none of it. "Please, Eric, just suck for a few minutes while I change Erica. I can't possibly hold you and change her. I don't have enough arms."

"I think our troubles are almost over." Cal appeared beside her and reached for Erica. "I'll change her. You handle Eric."

"Charley called?" Annie picked Eric up, and he stopped crying instantly.

"Yep." Cal lifted Erica high in the air and was rewarded with a big smile. "That was your mommy on the phone. She and your daddy are madly in love again and on their way to Las Vegas to get married."

"Vegas?" Annie cuddled Eric closer. "What about the twins?"

"They're going, too. I told Charley we'd fly them out and stay for the ceremony."

Annie sank onto the bed. "We're taking the twins to Las Vegas?"

"Sure. They can't miss the wedding, and neither can we. Charley and Rick are my best friends. Don't you want to see the babies' parents tie the knot?"

"Yes, but what about the campaign . . . the Board meeting?"

"We can take off a couple of days." He put Erica on the bed and began changing her diaper. "We deserve a reward for all our hard work, Annie. Besides, we don't have anything scheduled."

"No, not until next week, but—"

Cal looked at her and smiled. "Didn't I promise you a fantasy?" Before she could answer he continued, "We'll have it, Annie. We'll have our fantasy in Vegas after we hand over the babies."

10

ERIC LET OUT A LOUD, piercing yell and the flight attendant came flying down the aisle. They were scheduled to land in Vegas in less than an hour, and while Erica nestled in Annie's arms, sleeping soundly, Eric was another matter. He was ready to land *now*.

"Is the baby all right?" the stewardess asked. "Can I get you anything?"

"Just get us to Vegas," Cal replied, and Annie stifled a giggle.

An elderly man across the aisle didn't seem amused. He took off his wire-framed glasses and stared directly at Cal with a withering look. "Quiet, please," he commanded.

Then from the seat behind, a large woman tapped Cal on the shoulder. "It's the pressure," she said. "Give him a bottle."

Eric yelled again, mightily.

"Shut him up," the bespectacled man ordered.

Cal glanced over at Annie, but she just shrugged, indicating that he was on his own.

"Maybe he needs changing," the flight attendant offered.

Eric kept on yelling.

Before the woman behind them could add another suggestion, Cal stood up, cuddling Eric close. "Out of my way everyone, we're going for a walk," he announced as he started down the aisle toward the back of the plane.

Throughout the whole scene, Annie had sat silently, holding the sleeping Erica, trying not to laugh.

Finally, Eric's crying sputtered out and then ceased. Everything returned to normal as newspapers, magazines and books were picked up and passengers settled back into their own worlds, the little airplane drama over.

Cal, holding an exhausted, soundly sleeping Eric, slipped back into his seat. "I should have bought out all of first class," he grumbled. "Our babies have as much right on this plane as anyone."

Suddenly Annie began to laugh uncontrollably.

"Shh," Cal ordered. "You'll wake him."

"I can't help it," she managed between gasps. "It's so funny."

"All right, I give up. *What's* so funny?"

"You."

"Me?"

Annie started laughing again. "Yes, you, the man who doesn't approve of babies on airplanes. Remember our trip back from the Keys?"

He nodded. "That seems like a hundred years ago. A lot has changed. Besides, these are *our* babies—I mean—hell, you know what I mean." He shifted Eric to the other arm and leaned over to give the sleeping Erica a soft kiss on her forehead.

Then he looked up at Annie. "Once you get attached to them, you begin to feel protective."

Annie smiled and looked out the window. The plane was on its approach to the Vegas airport. "Not much longer. I wonder if Charley and Rick will pick us up?"

"You can count on it," Cal answered. "Rick is hot to see the babies."

Annie's eyes, shining with tears, met Cal's. "They won't be ours much longer."

Cal took her hand and squeezed it hard. "I know, Annie, I know."

THE MOMENT THEY STEPPED off the plane at McCarran International Airport, Annie was overcome by sights and sounds so amazing she almost forgot her sadness over the babies. She'd never seen a slot machine in her life; now she saw them everywhere she looked.

"Even at the airport?" she asked Cal as they stepped onto the moving walkway. The terminal was ablaze with ads for hotels and casinos. "Look at that— whoops," she said, clutching Erica and grabbing the handrail.

"Vegas is like no place in the world. And this is only the airport. Wait till you see The Strip. And the theme parks."

"Theme parks? You mean like Disneyland?"

"Just about. It's another world," Cal told her. "You'll be surprised."

But the big surprise was just ahead. As they stepped onto solid ground, a tall blond woman rushed toward them, her hair swirling around her shoulders, her long legs encased in geometric-patterned multicolored tights.

"Charley," Cal told her unnecessarily, "and that's Rick behind her, closing in fast."

Rick was stocky, hair pulled back in a ponytail, face red with excitement.

Charley was on them like a whirlwind, hugging the babies, kissing Cal, even kissing Annie, and dancing in her joy. Both babies were startled awake by the commotion. Erica clung to Annie, and Eric began to scream.

"This is your son, pal, say hello," Cal said to Rick. "Or maybe you'd like to start with the girl baby."

"Yep. I'll start with Erica," Rick decided, tentatively approaching the baby from behind, over Annie's shoulder. "By the way, I'm Rick," he said to Annie.

"Hi, Rick. Meet your daughter."

Not unexpectedly, Erica gave her father the look reserved for strangers, mouth turned down, bottom lip trembling. "I don't think she likes me, and the boy really hates me," Rick decided.

"Don't be silly, darling," Charley said as she gathered Eric into her arms, silencing his cries. "It just takes a little time."

Cal laughed. "Try again, Rick."

"Hello, baby," Rick attempted.

"Look at those eyes, darling. Isn't she beautiful?" Charley said warmly.

"Yes, very beautiful."

"Give her a kiss," Charley prompted.

"Okay. I'll just give her a little kiss," Rick said to Annie as he leaned over awkwardly and planted a quick kiss on top of the baby's head.

"She won't break. Pick her up, darling."

"No, I don't think I could...."

"Sure you can," Cal prompted.

"Just do like this. Watch . . ." Charley demonstrated with Eric, settling the baby in the crook of her arm.

Tentatively, Rick allowed Annie to hand Erica over.

Annie stepped back. She made herself smile as she watched Erica's father get to know his baby for the first time. It was a touching scene. And a terribly sad one. In the space of a few short minutes, Annie had experienced a whole range of emotions, from a kind of vindication when Eric screamed and Erica pouted at the sight of her father, followed by a touch of sadness when Erica finally went to her father.

After all, the babies belonged not to her and Cal but to their parents. She berated herself silently but couldn't stem the sadness. Especially as she watched the happy parents with their babies.

Finally, leaning on Cal, she said softly, "Let's go, please."

"But you can't leave," Charley said, overhearing the plea. "We want you both to join us for dinner and talk about the wedding."

"Nope," Cal said firmly. "It's been a long trip, and we're going to the hotel to collapse."

A frown creased Charley's perfect forehead. "But you will be in the wedding, won't you? We're expecting you to be best man and maid of honor, aren't we, darling?"

Rick stopped cooing at Erica long enough to agree. "Cal, my pal, I never would consider another best man. And from what Charley tells me, we owe thanks to you for helping out, Annie. So you will be in the wedding, won't you?"

Annie attempted unsuccessfully to hide her surprise. "What about all of your friends—"

"Oh, they'll be here. Everyone's flying to Vegas," Charley said. "But I want you and Cal in our wedding. For very special reasons. For the babies."

"Maybe I should stay with the babies during the ceremony," Annie offered.

"Oh, no," Charley laughed. "They're coming to the ceremony. I have new little outfits. Wait till you see them. They're going to look like little angels. Now, say you'll both be there for us."

Annie and Cal looked at each other. "Sure," Cal said, "wouldn't miss the opportunity."

"You'll need a dress, Annie. Did you bring anything?" Not waiting for an answer, Charley continued, "I'm wearing pale yellow so maybe something pastel. You'll look beautiful in a soft matching color. Pick out anything you want and charge it to me."

Clearly, Charley still loved to give orders, and Annie realized there was nothing she could do but go along with the beautiful, bossy woman who wanted everyone on her side. "You've done a great job as Cal's image consultant, hasn't she, Rick? Check out his hair. Have you ever seen it so short? And how about that East Coast image?"

But it had finally hit Rick that he was a father, that baby Erica was his daughter and baby Eric was his son. He was busy kissing one and then the other, not too interested in Cal's image.

Charley laughed musically and called out for a porter. After finding one and hustling him off to collect the luggage, she led the way, carrying Eric. Rick followed with Erica, and Cal and Annie trailed behind with the baby paraphernalia.

"Come on," Charley called out, "we have a limo waiting."

"The queen and her court," Annie mumbled as the entourage swept across the terminal and through the doors to the waiting limo. She wasn't prepared for the brilliant glare of the setting sun—or the flash of cameras that greeted them. She grabbed Cal's arm and tried to pull him back inside. "The press—everywhere!"

"Sorry," Rick called over his shoulder. "They've been on our tails since we got here."

"They know about the twins?" Cal asked.

"And the wedding." Charley flashed one of her million-dollar smiles.

Then the press descended on them.

"Over here, Charley."

"Smile for the cameras."

"Show us the baby!"

Erica was fascinated by the hubbub and lights, but Eric hid his face, and Rick took over, trading babies so Charley and Erica could pose. Grudgingly, Annie noted that Rick was doing a good job in comforting his son. He seemed to have a natural flair for fatherhood. Her twinge of jealousy lasted only until she realized her attention should be on Cal, to keep him out of the limelight, sneak him into the limo—

It was too late. A reporter had recognized Cal.

"Cal Markam? What are you doing here, giving the bride away? Or just in Vegas for a little gambling?" he added with a slight smirk.

Charley took Cal's arm. "Cal Markam is our cupid! He made it possible for Rick and me to get together. Isn't he wonderful?" She stood on tiptoe and gave him a kiss.

Camera shutters clicked, and Annie groaned. Short of wrestling the cameras from the photographers' hands, there was nothing she could do. She'd deal with the fallout from those photos tomorrow.

Then one of the reporters sidled up to Annie. "And who are you, honey? Part of this happy fairy tale?"

"No, I'm just the nanny. And I think my job is over."

ANNIE GAZED UP at the ceiling above the big round bed in their hotel room. "Unbelievable . . ." she murmured, but she'd been saying that almost constantly since they arrived in Vegas. She didn't know about the rest of the city, but The Strip, that long crazy street that *was* Las Vegas, had an aura of unreality. Sipping champagne during the ride from the airport, she'd let out her first gasp when they stopped at a light and Annie looked up to see the MGM Grand with its huge lion facade looming above them.

That was just the beginning. Darkness had fallen, and the whole world seemed illuminated as they drove past unbelievable hotels. The Luxor, an Egyptian pyramid guarded by a ten-story sphinx. Excalibur, straight out of the Middle Ages. The Mirage, complete with its own volcano.

But it was the advertised prices that boggled Annie's mind. "Could that hotel be only fifty dollars?" she asked. "It's not possible. But look, that one's thirty-five dollars! Cal, what's going on in this town?"

"It's Las Vegas."

"That's what you keep saying, but no hotel can make money charging thirty-five dollars a room."

"Oh, innocent Annie," he told her. "They make some of it up on the shows, headlined by name stars. But the big money's made in the casinos."

"Are you saying a couple comes here, pays practically nothing for a hotel room and then loses the difference gambling?"

Cal laughed. "More than the difference. Some people win. A few win big. Most of them lose. And some lose hugely. Meanwhile, the shows go on and the drinks flow. You also have to remember, Annie, that there are literally thousands of rooms in these hotels. It adds up. And of course, there are the slot machines."

"Of course," Annie agreed, shaking her head in wonder.

The wonder continued when they arrived at their hotel—the Roman Holiday. Annie held fast to Cal's arm as they were surrounded by people in togas, swooping down, taking their bags, checking them in, ushering them across marble floors, past splashing fountains and Corinthian columns into the frescoed elevator—all the while accompanied by a sound that was becoming familiar, the clanking of slot machines and the occasional jingle of coins as someone hit the jackpot.

After stepping off the elevators, they headed down grape-arbored hallways to their room.

"Yes, unbelievable," Annie repeated as she stretched in the huge round bed in the middle of their enormous bedroom. She'd managed to doze off at Cal's suggestion. Now, an hour later, she yawned, then called out, "Cal, are you in this Roman villa somewhere?"

He came in from the living room. "I'm here, and all the toga people are gone."

"Thank heavens." She raised her head and asked, "What time are the chariot races?"

Cal laughed as he tossed a couple of packages onto the bed, kicked off his shoes and dropped down beside her. "Actually, I think there really are—"

"No! Don't tell me."

"They don't actually race, but they drive chariots through the lobby twice a day."

"Now I've heard everything."

"We missed the early show," he said, looking at his watch, "but we can catch the next one—"

"I'll use my imagination," Annie said. "I don't think I could handle seeing it live."

"Good," he answered. "Because I've arranged with room service for a Roman banquet. It'll arrive a little later. Meanwhile, you and I are going to relax and not think about the babies."

Annie felt suddenly sad.

"Don't worry, we'll see them tomorrow. Tonight is just for us, as I promised."

"Okay, no baby talk tonight," she agreed. "I'm just as glad the babies aren't here to see all this—" She gestured around the room but didn't indicate the ceiling, which Cal hadn't seen.

Then he looked up and began to laugh.

"Kind of gets your attention, doesn't it?" Annie asked. "Satyrs and nymphs and fauns—"

"And nubile young females in some sort of sexual daisy chain. Very arousing. I wonder how they get in those positions? We'll just have to find out, won't we?"

he said slyly, rolling over, taking her in his arms, and kissing her thoroughly. "Oh, Annie, this is our night of nights."

As he kept one arm firmly around her, he grappled around with his other hand for one of the packages. "Open this."

Annie sat up. "You've been shopping?"

"There are shops in the hotel, Annie. Remember? It's Vegas."

Laughing, Annie opened the package and pulled the shimmering red satin nightie out of its bag. "Wow!"

Cal smiled in pleasure. "I thought we'd ditch the flannel nightie at least for tonight."

"I didn't even bring it! Didn't seem appropriate for Vegas," she joked. "But this—" She rubbed the satiny material against her face. "It's divine. Thank you so much." She had a sudden thought. "I'll put it on now."

"Not yet," he said. "Take it off, but don't put it on."

"What?"

Cal grinned. "Get undressed. I have another surprise." He pulled Annie to her feet. "The Roman baths. Have you seen them?"

"Here, in our suite?"

"Yep. Through that door. Marble hot tub with steaming foamy water, towels an inch thick—"

"I'm on the way," Annie said, unbuttoning her blouse. "And oh, Cal, bring the champagne Charley and Rick gave us, would you?"

"What? You want me to be your slave?" he asked and then answered himself. "Why not? When in Rome . . ."

When he got to the Roman-columned bath with the champagne and a bowl of fruit, Annie was already in the tub, submerged to her shoulders, luxuriating in the rapidly pulsating water.

Cal tossed his shirt on the floor. "No fair. As your slave, I thought I'd get to undress you."

"Too late," she teased. "This is *my* fantasy."

He looked down at her. "You told me you didn't have fantasies."

Annie smiled slyly up at him. "Maybe I lied. Or maybe your fantasies gave me ideas."

"I hope so," he said fervently.

"No more talking," Annie ordered. "Get those clothes off now!"

Cal pulled off his boots and jeans. Then, standing naked before her, he bowed slightly and asked, "May I join you?"

"Yes, slave," she replied.

Cal sank into the water and gasped at the extreme heat. "It's always a surprise," he said.

"You've spent a lot of time in hot tubs?"

Cal laughed. "Oh, yes, Annie, in my other life—before I became your client. But for now, I'm your slave." He settled beside her on the low ledge, letting the jets of hot water pound into his back.

She got into the game. "But does the slave sit with his master?"

"Master?" he asked.

"Mistress . . . I mean—"

They both laughed. "Yes," he said, "at the Roman Holiday Hotel and Casino, the slave waits upon his—mistress—and then sits beside her." He reached over and touched her thigh. "Yes, just what I needed." He leaned down and kissed her shoulder.

"Do you think that's slave behavior?" she asked.

"First, I bring you champagne and fruit." Cal extracted the bottle from the cooler, poured two glasses and then dropped a ripe, red strawberry into each one.

Annie reached for the glass but he held it away from her. "Oh, no, not yet, Your . . . Your . . ."

"You may call me Empress of Rome," she decreed graciously.

"Your Empress," he said softly, "let me assist you." He held the glass to her lips. When she had taken a long sip, he pulled out the strawberry and offered it to her. Annie bit down, and rich, red juice stained her mouth. She ate the juicy strawberry as he watched, hungry, not for the fruit, but for Annie.

Cal covered her mouth with his, and the sensation was mind-boggling. Champagne, strawberries and Annie. As they kissed, visions cascaded through his mind: the first time he saw her, businesslike and tense . . . Annie in the hammock on Mango Key, soft and sensual . . . Annie in his bed, welcoming him, wild and free . . . Annie, the lovely, loving Annie with the babies.

Her tongue was hot and seeking against his, and Cal wanted her with a deep, aching need.

Annie gently pulled away and with teasing eyes watched him as she caressed his chest, stroking his nipples. Cal could feel his breath quicken and his heart pound rhythmically. He leaned over and tried to kiss her again. Annie pulled back. "You're very forward for a mere slave."

"Then tell me what to do. I have only one goal—to obey you totally."

Laughter danced in Annie's eyes. "Oh, I like that. Let's see . . . More champagne then, I think."

He lifted the glass to her lips and she drank deeply. Cal finished the champagne, not taking his eyes from her. She seemed to glow; her face was flushed, her eyes shining.

"Anything else, Empress?" he teased. "I do have certain interesting talents—"

"So I've heard," she said, nibbling on his shoulder. "Why don't you show me?"

"Your wish is my command." He slid his hand along the inside of her thigh, slowly, or as slowly as he could manage in his building excitement. With playful fingers, he caressed the area around her moist center, not touching her there, but teasing her. He smiled into her eyes as she lifted her body upward, moving toward his fingers until, finally, he touched the moistness and heard her gasp. At that moment he kissed her deeply, feeling her tremble beneath him.

The taste of champagne, the scent of strawberries, the feel of her warm, wet body—Cal's head reeled from the mixed sensations. He drew her closer, moved her onto his lap and felt her wrap her bare legs around him. Settling higher on the ledge, their torsos out of the water, he caressed the roundness of her breasts and lowered his head, taking one tight, hard nipple in his mouth.

Annie dug her nails into the wet flesh of his shoulders and bit down on the lobe of his ear. A little pain shot through him, exciting him even more. They were deep into this sensual game, each testing the other, pushing to the limits. His teeth on her breasts were playfully rough, but he could sense her excitement. He bit a little harder and she dug her nails deeper into his shoulders.

"My slave is getting out of control," she said breathlessly.

"And so is my Empress. You might leave marks on my shoulders."

"Don't worry. I'll kiss them better."

Cal couldn't control the flame of excitement lit by both her words and actions, and he responded by abruptly lifting her above him. The desire was too strong in him to slow down now.

Annie met his actions with an urgency of her own as she slid her hand along his erection and pressed it against her aching entrance. The hot water erupting all around them seemed to aggravate their need.

She opened to him, settling onto his hard shaft as he pushed up and into her. Their eyes locked, and they began to move, faster and faster, adding stronger and stronger waves to the hot, pulsating water.

Cal gasped in pleasure as he leaned back against the marble edge of the whirlpool, passion overwhelming him. He opened his eyes and saw an image far more arousing than any fresco. His eyes drank in the vision of Annie Valentine in the throes of ecstasy.

HOURS LATER, their dinner cart sat neglected beside the door. Annie's silk gown lay in a red puddle on the floor. Annie and Cal lounged in the center of the giant round bed, arms around each other, legs entwined.

"I promised you a fantasy," Cal said, running his hand along her thigh and hip. "Remember?"

"Oh, yes," Annie sighed. "I remember. Except what happened to us tonight was better than any fantasy. Oh, Cal, I love making love to you." His body was warm and pliant against hers, his muscles hard against her softness. She wanted to melt into him, dissolve, become part of him.

Cal snuggled closer. "Then by all means, let's keep the Empress happy. That's what I'm here for, after all, to meet every one of your needs—no matter how erotic. Just tell me what you want."

"Nothing exotic this time."

"Oh . . ." There was disappointment in Cal's voice.

"No, just a kiss. I want you to kiss me."

His mouth was on hers, soft and sweet. But the softness and sweetness couldn't last. The passion was too great. Once more, they were consumed by it.

Annie pressed against him. Her breasts were hot and heavy, and deep inside sexual need twisted and turned and overcame her, just as strongly as before. She would never get enough of him, Annie thought. Never, never, never.

Words formed in her mind, and she repeated them again and again. *I love you, Cal. I love you.* But she didn't speak the words aloud.

11

THE NEXT DAY was a whirlwind that began at seven in the morning with Cal pulling Annie out of bed. "Time for a swim!"

"Cal, you must be crazy! It's November. It's cold."

"No, it's not."

"When we got in last night, it was very chilly," Annie reminded him.

"That was last night and this—"

"I know," she interrupted. "This is Las Vegas."

"I was going to say that this is the desert, Annie. In the desert, it's cold at night and hot during the day. Come on, get into your bathing suit."

"I didn't bring one," she told him.

"Remember those packages I brought in last night?" He looked around the floor beside the bed. "There was the red nightgown, and where's the other one?" He stood up with a package in his hand and pulled out a tiny black bikini.

"I can't wear that!"

"Sure you can."

She did. They swam in the hotel's largest Romanesque pool, had breakfast poolside and then hit the casinos. They started at the slot machines.

"I'm going to set a limit for myself," Annie declared. "Four quarters and that's it."

Twelve quarters later, Annie had won only once—a "jackpot" of six quarters, and lost the rest. "Okay, I'm down $1.50," she said.

"You can play on credit, Annie," Cal suggested with a laugh.

"Oh, no," she protested. "But how about blackjack?"

"Follow me."

At the green felt table she set a limit of ten dollars and lost it all—while Cal won eighty dollars.

"How did you do it?" she asked.

"Practice," he answered. "Chemin de fer, anyone?"

"Not me," Annie decided. "I'm going shopping while I still have money left. And aren't you supposed to help Rick choose wedding rings?"

"Yep. There's plenty of time. I have a little gambling to do first," he told her.

"Well, I'm off to find a bridesmaid's dress and to check the morning papers. I hate to think what the press has done with our arrival at the airport."

Cal gave her a lingering kiss while the dealer watched disinterestedly. "We're on holiday, Annie. Remember."

"Sure, sure," she answered, returning the kiss, "But I'm still buying the papers."

"Then I'll see you back in our Roman villa," he whispered. "Save a little time for your slave before the wedding."

Annie smiled up at him. "Will you be there—or at the gambling tables?"

"Give me an hour. I'll be there." He kissed her again.

"So will I," she promised.

THE BOUTIQUE dressing room was piled high with discarded dresses—too short, too tight, too fussy, lacy or beribboned. As far as Annie was concerned, nothing seemed right.

A frustrated salesclerk appeared in the doorway with another armful of dresses. "This is about it, Ms. Valentine. You've tried on everything else in your size."

Annie pulled off a tight red dress that was entirely inappropriate and said, "Chose one, the best of the bunch. Whatever it is, I'll go with it."

The woman searched through the dresses, chose one, hung it on a hook and beat a hasty retreat.

"No wonder she got out of here," Annie mumbled to herself. "Flowers? Me in flowers?"

The dress was made of a thin gauzy material, imprinted with bouquets of wildflowers tied with trailing ribbons in soft pastels. Annie grimaced. It had the kind of look she usually avoided. But she might as well try it on. After all, this was Charley's wedding, not hers. And the dress did look like one a bridesmaid might wear.

She slipped it on. The skirt fell below her knees in a swirl of pale material. The neckline was rounded and low, but not too low. Just right for a wedding.

But a wedding in Vegas?

Maybe the short, tight, red number would be more suitable, Annie thought. Or something with feathers!

The clerk reappeared. "It's perfect," she said. "You look beautiful. So young and—"

"Stop right there," Annie interrupted. "I'll take it. Shoes are next."

"And maybe a hat, a nice summery picture hat with flowers."

"No," Annie answered firmly. "No hat. This Alice-in-Wonderland look is as far as I go."

Annie put her purchases on her credit card, even though Charley and Cal had both offered to pick up the tab. She was a working woman and could pay her own way. Or at least she *used* to be a working woman. It had been a long time since she'd been in her office or even thought about business.

She stopped on the way back to the hotel for a cup of coffee at a little bakery that didn't seem to have the usual Las Vegas look. But there were the slot machines, as always. With a shrug, Annie fed a quarter into the most likely-looking winner. Then another quarter.

"I'm stopping at four," she told herself as a mixture of fruits came up another time. "Just lemons," she demanded, "only lemons." Another loss and she threw up her hands. She invested her last quarter in a newspaper and sat down to drink the coffee—and find out what damage had been done by the press.

There they were on the front page, Charley and Erica and Cal, with Rick nowhere to be seen. At first glance they appeared to be a happy couple, reunited at last. Mommy. Daddy. Baby. Annie's heart sank. How many papers, she wondered, would pick up the photo and miss the real story?

She read the caption.

"He's my cupid," super model Charley
    Baird says of old friend Cal Markam. "He

made it possible for me to reunite with
Rick." Baird and Rick Johnson, the parents of
four-month-old twins, will be married
in Las Vegas this week.

That was better, Annie decided. The real story, if
anyone bothered to read it. She paid for her coffee and
asked the waitress for directions to the nearest photo-
copy center.

THE WHITE STRETCH LIMO was filled with Annie's bil-
lowing dress, a bottle of champagne on ice, stacks of
presents for the bride and groom, and—in the middle
of it all—Annie and Cal laughing happily.

"It's been a great eighteen hours," Cal said, planting
a kiss on Annie's cheek.

Annie agreed with a smile, without mentioning the
only sad note, losing the babies, who would be going
off to California with their parents.

"I know," Cal said, reading her mind. "I'll miss them
too, but life goes on, and we might as well enjoy it." He
grinned. "I've managed to so far, and I don't expect today to be an exception."

In fact, Annie had enjoyed herself for the past eighteen hours, too. They'd been among the happiest hours
of her life. It was ironic, she mused. She'd been hired
to change Cal, but she was the one who'd ended up
changing the most. She'd finally learned what was important—not the destination, but the journey to get
there, no matter how bumpy, winding or twisted.

She'd found pleasure in the spontaneous and unexpected. Just like this crazy wedding. Although she ex-

pected it to be a little tacky—a Las Vegas event filled with Surfer Babes and Dudes. Also, since most of the guests would be old friends of Cal's, she couldn't help wondering how he would react to it all.

When they stopped in front of the Hearts and Flowers Wedding Chapel, she was totally surprised. The building was right out of a quaint New England village, its white clapboards gleaming in the sun, the ornate Victorian wood trim fresh and shining. Masses of potted flowers flanked the stairs, and in the small garden there was a heart-shaped trellis and a scattering of heart-shaped benches.

"It's lovely," she said, her voice betraying amazement.

Cal took her arm and guided her up the steps. "So what were you expecting, neon lights and an Elvis impersonator giving the bride away?"

"Something like that," Annie admitted. Now she was glad she'd opted for a conservative dress. This wedding was going to be more traditional than she'd imagined.

A young man, impeccably dressed in tails and white tie intercepted them at the entrance. "Baird-Johnson party? Two o'clock?"

"Best man and maid of honor," Cal announced.

"If the gentleman will meet the groom in the silver room..." He gestured with a gloved hand. "I'll escort the lady to the gold room."

Cal kissed Annie lightly on the forehead. "That sounds like an order. See you in church."

Charley was ensconced in the gold room, wearing a bright yellow silk dressing gown and a head full of curlers, surrounded by a cadre of helpers. But Annie's attention wasn't on the bride. She headed straight for the twins, propped up on a big sofa.

"Oh, my babies," she said softly, dropping to her knees so their faces were on her level. "I missed you so much."

Eric didn't seem particularly pleased to see her, but Erica gurgled and flashed a smile that melted Annie's heart. "Now Eric, what about you? Don't you know who I am?" She held out her hand, and Eric grabbed a finger with a happy shriek.

"They know me," Annie cried. "They remember!"

"Well, of course, they remember," Charley called out. "You were their temporary mom." She shooed away the makeup man, hairstylist and manicurist and flopped down beside Annie, giving her a big hug. No tentative, for-the-cameras hug, but a genuine squeeze from the heart.

"I can't thank you enough for all you've done."

Annie didn't know what to say. Finally, she came up with, "I love the twins."

"I know you do, and I want you and Cal to feel free to visit them anytime. You'll always be welcome."

"I might take you up on that," Annie replied. "They've really captured a piece of my heart. In fact, I don't think I'll ever be the same."

"That's the trouble with babies," Charley said lightly. "They have a way of rearranging your life. Don't you, kids?" She gave them each a kiss. "How do you like their outfits? I decided that since the bride wasn't wearing white, the babies might as well. I think the white eyelet lace dress looks darling on Erica, but do you think it's a little too much for Eric to be in a matching shirt?"

"Not at all," Annie declared. "And the white linen pants are very chic."

Charley laughed. "I think so, too. And I gave him blue socks and Erica pink ones, so there'd be no doubt who's the boy and who's the girl."

"They look like angels," Annie said.

"Which we know they're not, but..." Charley laughed again and got to her feet. Waiting without complaint, her helpers held up the pale yellow chiffon wedding dress, all prepared for her to step into it, which she finally did, creating a whirl of excitement.

Then she stood patiently while she was zipped, buttoned and readjusted, the curlers removed and hair combed out, her makeup freshened. Her hair was twisted with blossoms of delicate white-and-yellow orchids into a braid. The effect was amazing, Annie thought, innocent and sexy at the same time.

"You look beautiful," Annie said, admiring the dress with its high collar, lacy cuffs and flowing sleeves.

"My bouquet has these same orchids," Charley said, tossing her thick, braided hair. "They're so sweet and demure—not at all like me." She caught Annie's eye in the mirror and winked. "Remember, most of what I do is for show, for my image as Charley. The real Charlotte is a devoted mom and will be a great wife. Don't worry about the babies."

"I won't," Annie promised, still a little sad but not worried about what kind of mother they had.

Charley stood up and reached for her bouquet, studying herself critically in the full-length mirror. "A tiny bit more blush," she suggested to the makeup man, "and the dress seems to be hanging a little crooked in back, and one of the orchids is slipping and . . ."

Assistants scurried to take care of the problems, and once more Annie was reminded of a queen, except this time she saw Charley in a slightly different light. She liked what she saw. It was funny, Annie thought, that since she'd met Cal everything in her life seemed to have been turned upside down. Even her opinions.

"We're almost ready," Charley announced. "The wedding chapel is gorgeous. I've had it filled with flowers, orchids, lilies and roses, and about fifty of our friends have flown in from L.A. The party is going to be fabulous. Have you met any other friends of Cal's?"

"No, just you and Rick," Annie admitted. "I've only been involved in Cal's business life, his image, his—"

Charley's musical laugh rang out again. The twins heard her and chortled along with their mother. "Remember, I've seen you together, Annie. You're a great twosome."

"Oh, no," Annie denied. "No, we're not—"

"Annie . . ." Charley cautioned. "Sparks fly between you two—and not just when you're arguing! You're a team."

"Well. He's teamed up with a lot of women before me." Those words just came out. She hadn't meant to bring up Cal's past.

Charley adjusted her braid and looked at Annie curiously. "Sure, that's true. Women have always flocked around Cal. But that was then. This is now. *You're* now," she added, giving Annie a hug. "We're in today. Don't worry about yesterday."

"I don't," Annie lied. "Not a bit." But everything about Cal's old life *did* bother her, everything about yesterday *did* worry her. And today, yesterday would return in the form of all of Cal's friends.

She forced a smile, reminding herself that today was all about Charley and Rick, not Annie and Cal. "Is there anything special I'm supposed to do, like carry a bouquet or say something—"

Charley looked at her, eyes widening in surprise. "You mean Cal didn't tell you? That devil! I guess he wanted to surprise you. Why, honey, our best man and maid of honor are going to be the baby bearers."

"The baby... what?"

"You've heard of ring bearers? Well, instead of rings, you and Cal will each carry a baby. You didn't think I'd get married without them, did you?"

"No, but I thought they'd be sitting with your guests, in someone's lap."

"Not on your life," Charley objected. "And there is absolutely no one I'd entrust the twins to except you and Cal. You're their second parents."

Annie burst into laughter. "So that's why you were so insistent about us being in your wedding. Charley, you're amazing!"

"I know," she said complacently. "Rick tells me that all the time. Now, I think you should carry Eric, and Cal, Erica. So it's girl, boy, girl, boy. How does that sound?"

Annie remembered that evening in bed when she and Cal and the babies slept in a row. She smiled to herself. "Yes, that sounds great. Girl, boy, girl, boy. Just perfect."

THE WEDDING was beautiful, the bride radiant, and the babies perfectly behaved in the arms of their familiar baby-sitters, Annie thought proudly as the wedding party adjourned to the Roman Holiday Hotel for the reception.

It was almost as elegant as the ceremony itself. Charley had turned the hotel's Bacchanal Room from the usual Roman-orgy look into a spring garden. Annie wound her way through statues of fauns and satyrs, nymphs and dryads, all draped in garlands of flowers, to the end of the room. There she watched as the toga-clad waiters and waitresses, laden with trays, passed among the crowd, adding an atmosphere of classicism to the party.

But amid the music, laughter, fine champagne and hors d'oeuvres—everything to make a party successful—she stood beside the statue of a water nymph, feeling as low as she had ever felt in her life. She looked across the room at Cal. He was holding Erica in the crook of one arm and had the other around the slim waist of a tall redhead. A group of friends surrounded him, laughing and talking, their faces radiating good cheer.

Annie had been introduced to most of them, but the names and faces had come and gone in a blur. Megan, who had something to do with television...Scott, who owned a surfboard retail shop...Jill, who'd just signed a contract as spokeswoman for a new swimwear line...Mac, a top money manager...and Lisa, former Surfer Babe, now aspiring actress. They'd been polite to Annie before turning their attention back to Cal. She'd tried to be gay, but all the while she felt a little like Cal's *femme du jour*, just one girlfriend in a long line of them. One who didn't fit into either of Cal's worlds, not staid Philadelphia or freewheeling California.

Suddenly Annie became aware of male voices from the other side of the statue. They were laughing, joking, a little tipsy.

"Cal looks like he's back in the groove," the first voice said. "And not altogether unhappy to have Kim beside him."

"Well, you know Cal's style," the other voice declared, "here today, gone tomorrow."

Annie shuddered at the echo of her own thoughts.

When the laughter subsided, the first voice went on, "He looks pretty glad to be back with the old crowd and away from life in Philadelphia. Must be a drag, keeping up that Mr. Nice Guy image."

"Do you believe for a moment he's going to take over the family business after Surfer Babes and Dudes and Bikini Kleen?"

"He'll probably give it a go, beat the odds and move on. I heard him wheeling and dealing just now, sorting out a couple of new possibilities."

"Yeah, the really hot one is that string of resorts from San Diego all the way down the Baja peninsula. The Mexican peninsula is a developer's dream, and if anybody can make it happen, it's Cal. If he goes for it, I might even buy into that deal."

Annie had heard enough, and she moved away, her eyes still on Cal, who had never looked happier. He was in his element, laughing and joking with his friends, relaxed, secure, the center of attention—and maybe making a deal that would return him to California and his old life.

Absorbed in her thoughts, puzzled and upset, she almost ran into Rick.

"Whoops. Oh, it's you, Annie. Having a good time, I hope," he said merrily.

"Yes, it's a lovely party," she replied.

"Looks like Cal's enjoying himself, too. It's great to have him back."

"Have him back?"

"Well, for a while, anyway. I know he's got to do that gig in Philly—"

"It's not exactly a gig, Rick. He's going to be taking over the family business. It'll be quite a challenge for him." Annie realized that she was trying to convince herself, as well as Rick, that this was really Cal's ultimate goal, that there weren't any other "deals" in the picture.

"Oh, sure. Cal likes challenges. That's his way of operating, really. Find an impossible situation. Take it on. Beat the odds and move to the next one. Nobody thought Bikini Kleen would make it—and look what happened. He likes to straighten things out."

"Markam Investments needs some straightening out, too," Annie said, a little weakly. "That's why it's important for Cal to get past the Board."

"Oh, he'll do it, Annie," Rick said, giving her a big bear hug. "I'm sure the idea really appeals to him."

"Yes, it does," Annie agreed, glad he seemed to understand.

"Yeah. A company that needs to be turned around, a hostile board, impossible odds. Cal can do it."

"I know he can." Annie brightened a little.

"He'll enjoy the success for a while and then move on, looking for something new. That's Cal. He's like that with women, too, he—" Rick broke off in midsentence and had the grace to look embarrassed. "Don't mind me, Annie. I've had a little too much champagne. My wedding day and all that, you know." He gave her another hug. "It's not my business to speculate on Cal's future. He's changed a lot. We all have. Just look at me and Charley, a married couple with two kids. Who would ever have thought?"

Rick was obviously trying to make Annie feel better and even though it wasn't working, she couldn't act morose on his wedding day.

"Your wife is some gal," she said as cheerily as she could manage.

They both looked across the dance floor at Charley, twirling from the arms of one guest to another. Cal had just cut in on her, and they danced a slow waltz with baby Erica between them while another guest held Eric up to watch.

"Yep, some gal," Rick agreed.

"And very surprising," Annie went on honestly. "Not always what you think."

Rick laughed. "I never thought of twins, for one thing—or two things, I should say. By the way, Annie, thanks again for taking care of the babies for us. That gave Charley and me a chance to put our relationship back together and get ready for our new life."

"I guess it'll be quite a change when one of the hottest models in America settles down to family life."

"Charley can always go back to work if she wants to," Rick said. "I can take care of the kids. But for a few months both of us are going to take a holiday while I get to know Eric and Erica." Rick smiled broadly. "They're some cute babies, aren't they?"

Annie had no problem agreeing with that. "The cutest babies I've ever seen."

Her eyes sought Cal again. He was standing with one of the hotel staff, listening attentively. Then he looked around, saw Annie, and gestured to her. She made her excuses to Rick and quickly followed Cal out of the Bacchanal Room, concerned about the expression she'd seen on his face.

"What is it?" she asked when she caught up with him.

"Dad. He wouldn't be calling unless it was important."

Cal took the call at the desk, and Annie stood by, trying to make sense of his monosyllabic responses.

He listened for a long moment, frowning, before responding. "Yes, sir. I think you're right. This is the showdown, and I need to be there. We'll try to fly out on the red-eye tonight to get there for tomorrow morning's meeting."

Another word or two and he hung up, turning to Annie.

"Trouble?" she asked.

"It could be. Seems Aunt Dee has decided to strike now. She's called an emergency Board meeting."

"Oh, no. Why?"

"She thinks my involvement with Charley, two babies and a Vegas wedding is the last straw. It's 'unseemly,'" he said, managing a grin. "Only Dee would use a word like that. Anyhow, it looks like this is going to be the moment of reckoning, when the Board members choose sides. Either I'm in or I'm out—"

Annie's mind worked frantically. She glanced at her watch. "We still might be able to get into some of the morning papers back east. I can make a few calls, give this wedding thing a positive spin—how you single-handedly brought Rick and Charley together, how you took care of their babies, how it was all your idea—"

"No, Annie," he said firmly. "Leave it alone. You've done all you can for me, and I'm on my own now."

"But—"

"No arguing." He looked down at her, his face as serious as she'd ever seen it. "You know me well enough by now to know that I'm always going to stir things up. You've done your best, but I'll never be able to stay out of trouble."

"That's not true," she argued. "You've been very—"

"Annie, please. The Board needs to realize who I am. If they can't deal with Charley and the twins, maybe I'm not the guy for them."

Annie didn't say anything more. Her heart was sinking.

"Come on," he said, reaching for her hand. "Let's get our tickets changed and pack up." He held on to her hand, but he seemed preoccupied, as if his mind were already racing ahead—leaving thoughts of her far behind.

12

EXHAUSTION HIT ANNIE as soon as the plane took off.
She felt wrung out and let down. Closing her eyes, she
sank back in her seat and tried to organize hopelessly
erratic thoughts. There was so much she needed to discuss with Cal. Was he still determined to take over
Markam? Or had the lure of his old life hooked him?
Was he really ready for confrontation with the Board
and Dee? Or was all the pretense of change no longer
worthwhile to him? After all, he believed he really
hadn't changed at all.

To Annie, he had changed. But Rick, Charley and
their friends didn't think so. Who was right?

She glanced at Cal out of the corner of her eye. His
handsome, finely chiseled profile was serious, almost
stern, against the dark window of the plane. He looked
lost in thought, as if he didn't want to be disturbed.

But Annie needed to talk. She moved obliquely into
the conversation. "I miss the babies, don't you? I hope
they're all right."

"I miss them, too, but I'm sure they're fine. After all,
they're exactly where they need to be."

Annie bit her lip and took a deep breath before
plunging into the next topic. "What about you, Cal?
Are you where you want to be?" she asked softly.

"What do you mean?"

She forged ahead. "Do you want to be flying back to Philadelphia? Or would you rather be in California? I understand your friends had some great deals to offer."

"They always do." He gazed at Annie. "And some of them are awfully appealing."

"And dealing with the Markam Board, trying to change your life, hasn't been as easy as you thought. Or as much fun," she offered, studying his face intently.

"Nothing is easy," he equivocated.

"You're almost there, Cal," she urged. "You're so close. Everything is coming together. And I've figured out how to handle this baby thing. I made copies of the photo in the Vegas newspaper—including the caption which explains everything. In it, Charley calls you a cupid. You're a hero, Cal, and the Board will love it."

He smiled, almost sadly, Annie thought. A chill of apprehension ran through her.

"I'm going to deal with the Board my way, Annie. Not your way—or Dad's."

"Oh, Cal," she begged, for herself as much as for him. "Please don't do anything foolish."

"I'm always foolish, Annie." His eyes were tired, but there was a flicker of the old, teasing Cal in them. "We should both rest. God knows we'll need all our energy to face the Board."

"We?"

"Yep. I want you with me."

"But I can't. Someone might connect me with Bert's firm, and your Aunt Dee—"

"I want you there, Annie. It's important. I'll have things to say that you need to hear."

To Annie, that sounded ominous, and she was afraid, not only for Cal's future with Markam, but for their future together.

But it was Cal's show from now on. Annie had no control over what was going to happen, and the feeling left her shaken and scared. She knew that she had everything to lose . . . including Cal.

ANNIE STOPPED BY her apartment briefly, showered and changed in a space that seemed strangely lonely without the babies. Then she headed for Markam Enterprises. Her fears hadn't abated by the time she got to the building. But she knew that no matter what happened, what choices Cal made, she would support him.

Cal and his father were standing face-to-face in the entrance of the boardroom when Annie appeared in the doorway. She found out immediately what the younger man's intentions were.

"I'm fighting for this job, Dad," Cal told his father. "And I need Annie with me." He looked serious, resolute and very determined. Annie suspected that nothing but Cal's ruthless determination could persuade J.C. to take his son seriously.

"Most irregular," J.C. complained. "No offense to you, Ms. Valentine." He glanced at her. "I'm grateful for all your help, but this isn't usually done."

"This is not a usual Board meeting," Cal replied. "You're the chairman. You can do it, Dad. So do it."

The two men stared at each other for a long moment, and then J.C. looked away. "My God, son, you are a Markam, heart and soul. I like that. Come on in,

Ms. Valentine," he said with a courtly little half bow. "Soon as I put out this cigar, I'll find a place for you."

Annie was led to a leather chair at the big oval table. Cal sat on his father's right, his face serious. He'd made his decision to fight for the job as head of Markam Investments, and Annie could tell he was ready for the battle. As she had promised herself, she was ready to help—no matter what came next for her and Cal. She pulled out the clipping from the Las Vegas paper and scribbled a note to Mr. Markam— This tells the whole story, in case you need it.

She placed the clipping in a file folder and passed it to J.C. He looked confused for a moment before opening the file. His eyes skimmed the clipping, then he looked back at her with what she could have sworn was a wink.

Annie settled back, aware of another pair of eyes on her. She was under the close scrutiny of Dee Frame. She knew Cal's aunt recognized her and was trying to fit the pieces together.

"I think it's time for us to begin," J.C. announced as he stood up. "Since this is a special meeting, called by six of our ten members, we'll dispense with reading the minutes and go right to the heart of the issue."

Annie's own heart sank. Dee had rallied five other members, which meant a majority of the Board was on her side.

"One moment, please." Dee's well-bred voice broke in. "There's someone here who has nothing to do with Markam Investments or this meeting."

J.C. shot his sister an icy look. "You're incorrect, Dee, as you will soon find out."

"But—"

"I'm in charge here. Ms. Valentine is acting as my special assistant, and I believe that is covered in the by-laws. Any other questions or comments?" His cool blue eyes flicked around the table. "I thought not."

Annie tried to suppress her smile. J.C. was as smooth as silk and twice as slippery. She looked at Cal, whose face was deep in concentration, and wished she had a clue as to what he was thinking.

"In front of you," J.C. said, "are folders containing material about my son, John Calvin Markam IV. As you know, it is my wish that he succeed me. The information is self-explanatory. The first pages contain his profit-and-loss sheets from California businesses. You will note," he added proudly, "all profit, no loss."

Annie studied the Board members closely as they thumbed through the pages. Five men, five women, all well into middle age; in fact, a few of them seemed to be in their eighties.

"The next pages," J.C. said, "are a compilation of my son's philanthropic efforts since he returned to Phila-delphia. They range from the environmental—"

"Alligators?" asked an elderly man with a short mil-itary haircut and ruddy complexion. "What's that all about?"

"Crocodiles," Cal corrected. "An endangered spe-cies." Without turning in his chair, he smiled in An-nie's direction.

A woman wearing a turban and a huge cape spoke up. "I adore animals. Have you been to our zoo, Cal? I'm on the Board there, and I—"

J.C. interrupted smoothly. "We all appreciate the importance of nature's creatures, and none more than Cal. But there's much more to his philanthropy. Notice his deep involvement with local charities, the cultural world, his generous donation of time and money to help wherever he can—including our local zoo." J.C. leaned back on his heels. "I daresay he is one of the most highly regarded young men in this city, a talented entrepreneur and a beloved philanthropist, who should be elected—by acclamation. I see no need to take a vote."

J.C. sat down to a smattering of applause. Good, Annie thought, some members were on their side. Then she saw Dee waving her hand, waiting to be recognized.

J.C. toyed with Dee, looking around the table. "Any response? Oh, Dee, do you have something to say?"

Dee rose to her feet. As usual, she was immaculately turned out in a bright turquoise suit and elegant jewelry, gold at her ears and neck, diamonds sparkling on her fingers.

"I have a great deal to say. In fact, I have a file of my own." She waved it in the air, and Annie groaned inwardly. "You all know how loyal I am to family." She smiled what Cal called the barracuda smile, baring her teeth. "And, after all, Cal is family, my beloved nephew."

Somehow, Annie noticed, Cal managed to keep a straight face.

"But something suspicious has been going on, and I feel obligated to share it with you. This young lady, Annie Valentine, introduced herself to me some days ago but said her name was Valenti and that she and Cal had . . . well, a personal relationship." Dee spoke those words delicately, as if they denoted something extremely sordid.

"Later I met Ms. Valenti or Valentine at the Markam town house. With a baby in her arms! She told me that the child was her cousin's, but the story sounded incredibly contrived. Naturally, I assumed at the time that the child in fact belonged to Cal . . ." She paused dramatically. "And Ms. Valentine."

As one, the Board members turned their gaze to Annie, who could do nothing but sit quietly, waiting while Dee's damaging speech ran her course. Cal could lose, Annie realized as Dee droned on. He could lose because of *her*! How could that happen when she loved him so much?

Dee was rummaging through her file. "But I was wrong about who the mother was." She held up a newspaper photo. "Here is the mystery child again, this time in the arms of the model, Charley Baird, in Las Vegas, and beside her—none other than Cal." Dee made an effort to soften her triumphant look.

With relief, Annie saw J.C. react, opening his own folder. Quickly, he was on his feet to face Dee, waving the article Annie had photocopied. "I have that same picture," he growled, "except mine has the whole story. This isn't Cal's baby. He was only helping out two of his friends, which points out again what a fine man he is, what friendship and loyalty mean to him."

"That is not the point," Dee interrupted. "The point is that this kind of publicity places Cal in a questionable position. Sneaking around, hiding and lying—

such actions only call attention to some of his less noble escapades. He can't outrun his past, no matter how much you wish he could, J.C. Now, as for this baby—"

"I've had enough," Cal said, surging to his feet. For a terrible instant Annie was afraid he was going to walk out. She held her breath, waiting.

"Give me the photos," he demanded, "both of them. Right now."

There was such command in his voice that Dee did as he asked.

"This is not the issue," he said, holding up the photos. "But for point of clarity, there are two babies, twin children of good friends, and they aren't a part of this discussion. They're far too special, and my feelings for them too personal to involve them in this kind of name-calling and street fighting."

Annie looked around the boardroom. No one spoke or even moved as Cal continued.

"The trouble with babies—" he began, and then stopped himself. "No, the great thing about babies is that they love you not because of your profit-and-loss sheet or your picture in the paper, but because of the care you give them, the kindness and gentleness that's given honestly, purely, without any artifice."

Annie had no idea what was coming next, and neither, she realized, did anyone else. They seemed fascinated and confused by Cal's words. All eyes were on him.

"So let's deal honestly with each other, here and now. I want this job. I can make the company more profitable than ever. Each of you knows I have the background and experience. But I can't succeed unless I have Board support. Unless you trust me."

Although he hadn't looked Annie's way, she didn't take her eyes off him.

"Since we're being honest, let's talk about all the good press I've gotten, none of which was my doing." He finally looked at her, intently. "It's all due to Annie Valentine, the very talented publicist whose job it was to get me in line and keep me there, to turn my image around and make me acceptable to the Board. And she did a hell of a job." He looked back at the Board members. "But that Cal Markam is her creation. I haven't changed at all."

There was a mumble of conversation up and down the table as all eyes swung toward Annie again. Unable to contain herself any longer, she got to her feet and stood beside Cal.

"Really," Dee said. "This is totally out of order!"

"I know," J.C. agreed, pounding his gavel to control the group. "But why not let her talk? Everyone else has."

"Hear, hear," someone shouted.

It took Annie a moment to catch her breath. When she finally started to speak her voice was shaky, but she gained confidence as she went along. "Maybe Cal is right. In many ways, he hasn't changed. But I don't think that's such a bad thing. He has always been loyal to his friends and strong in the face of adversity. He has always seen what needed to be done, and he's done it. And as for his escapades, as Mrs. Frame calls them—" Annie raised her chin defiantly and stared Dee down.

"Cal enjoys life more than anyone I know. And what, I ask you, is wrong with that?"

"Not one damned thing," an elderly bearded man called out. "Ought to have more of it."

The turbaned woman spoke up next. "I'd say it was very clever to hire Ms. Valentine. She did the job, didn't she? All of these stories reflect well on our company."

Encouraged, Annie continued. "Cal Markam is a good man," she said emphatically, "and even though he doesn't want to talk about the babies, I will. Their mother entrusted their lives to him, and he didn't fail them. He won't fail you either," she added in a strong voice.

Tears glittered in Annie's eyes. She hoped she wasn't going to cry, but just as the thought came to her, the tears began to roll down her cheeks.

Dee regarded her coldly. "I think we can ignore Ms. Valentine's emotional appeal. Obviously, she's in love with the man and her opinion can't be trusted."

All the frustration and uncertainty Annie had felt over the past weeks welled up inside her and took the form of anger. "Damn right," she blurted out. "I love him with all my heart. If anyone's life has been changed, it's mine—and for the better." There, she'd said it! Whatever the consequences, she'd bared her own heart for him—and everyone else—to see.

Cal's response was to hug her close and, with his arm wrapped around her, address the Board again. "I made a mistake when I said that I hadn't changed. Two little babies and one fabulous woman made me realize what was lacking in my life—and that was love. Love changes everything. Even me."

"So marry her," a wrinkled little lady dressed in black piped up joyfully. "And let her help you run the company."

"Good thinking, Mrs. Meriweather." Cal looked down at Annie and said quietly. "I was planning to ask you *after* the vote. If I lost—"

Annie stopped him and smiled through tears. "Win or lose, the answer is yes. Yes, I'll marry you!"

"I love you, Annie Valentine, more than anything in life." He kissed her then, long and hard.

The Board members burst into applause, some jumping to their feet. The ruddy-faced man shouted out, "This is the best damned meeting I've been to in forty years. To hell with procedure. I say vote Cal in and then let's have a party!"

J.C. pounded frantically with his gavel, and somehow order was restored and a vote taken. But Annie and Cal didn't even notice when John Calvin Markam IV was voted by acclamation the new head of Markam Investments. They were lost in their kiss and visions of their future.

Just the two of them for now.

And later . . . A baby. Or two.

Spoil yourself next month
with these four novels from

Temptation

IN PRAISE OF YOUNGER MEN by Lyn Ellis

Will Case was too big, far too attractive and much, much too
sexy. And for the next few months, he would be sharing a
cabin with Carolina. Will was also best friends with her little
brother—and the same age!

THE RELUCTANT HUNK by Lorna Michaels

Ariel Foster wanted Jeff McBride to do a series for her TV
station. She knew every woman in town would tune in to watch
the drop-dead gorgeous man, if only she could persuade him to
work for her. But she soon realised she wanted the reluctant
hunk for herself.

BACHELOR HUSBAND by Kate Hoffmann

Come live and love in L.A. with the tenants of Bachelors Arms.
The first in a captivating new mini-series.

Tru Hallihan lives in this trendy apartment block and has no
thoughts of settling down. But he can't resist a bet to date
popular radio presenter, Caroline Leighton. Caroline will only
co-operate at a price—Tru must pose as her husband for a day!

SECOND-HAND BRIDE by Roseanne Williams

Brynn had married Flint Wilder knowing he was on the
rebound from her twin sister, Laurel. Six months later, Brynn
had left Flint, fearing she'd never be more than a substitute for
her twin. Now Brynn was back in town and Flint seemed hell-
bent on making up. But could she ever be sure she wasn't just a
stand-in for her sister?